Books by

MW00366212

Historical Western Romance Series

MacLarens of Fire Mountain

Tougher than the Rest, Book One
Faster than the Rest, Book Two
Harder than the Rest, Book Three
Stronger than the Rest, Book Four
Deadlier than the Rest, Book Five
Wilder than the Rest, Book Six

Redemption Mountain

Redemption's Edge, Book One
Wildfire Creek, Book Two
Sunrise Ridge, Book Three
Dixie Moon, Book Four
Survivor Pass, Book Five
Promise Trail, Book Six
Deep River, Book Seven
Courage Canyon, Book Eight
Forsaken Falls, Book Nine
Solitude Gorge, Book Ten
Rogue Rapids, Book Eleven
Restless Wind, Coming next in the series!

MacLarens of Boundary Mountain

Colin's Quest, Book One,
Brodie's Gamble, Book Two
Quinn's Honor, Book Three
Sam's Legacy, Book Four
Heather's Choice, Book Five
Nate's Destiny, Book Six
Blaine's Wager, Book Seven
Fletcher's Pride, Book Eight
Bay's Desire, Book Nine
Cam's Hope, Book Ten, Coming next in the
series!

Contemporary Romance Series

MacLarens of Fire Mountain

Second Summer, Book One
Hard Landing, Book Two
One More Day, Book Three
All Your Nights, Book Four
Always Love You, Book Five
Hearts Don't Lie, Book Six
No Getting Over You, Book Seven
'Til the Sun Comes Up, Book Eight
Foolish Heart, Book Nine
Forever Love, Book Ten, Coming next in the
series!

Peregrine Bay

Reclaiming Love, Book One, A Novella
Our Kind of Love, Book Two

Burnt River

Shane's Burden, Book One by Peggy Henderson
Thorn's Journey, Book Two by Shirleen Davies
Aqua's Achilles, Book Three by Kate Cambridge
Ashley's Hope, Book Four by Amelia Adams
Harpur's Secret, Book Five by Kay P. Dawson
Mason's Rescue, Book Six by Peggy L.
Henderson
Del's Choice, Book Seven by Shirleen Davies
Ivy's Search, Book Eight by Kate Cambridge
Phoebe's Fate, Book Nine by Amelia Adams
Brody's Shelter, Book Ten by Kay P. Dawson
Boone's Surrender, Book Eleven by Shirleen
Davies
Watch for more books in the series!

The best way to stay in touch is to subscribe to my newsletter.
Go to www.shirleendavies.com and subscribe in the box at the top of the right column that asks for your email. You'll be notified of new books before they are released, have chances to win great prizes, and receive other subscriber-only specials.

Bay's Desire

MacLarens of Boundary Mountain

Historical Western Romance Series

SHIRLEEN DAVIES

Book Nine in the MacLarens of Boundary Mountain

Historical Western Romance Series

Avalanche Ranch Press, LLC
PO Box 12618
Prescott, AZ 86304

Book design and conversions by Joseph Murray at 3rdplanetpublishing.com

Cover design by Kim Killion, The Killion Group

ISBN: 978-1-941786-91-8

I care about quality, so if you find something in error, please contact me via email at
shirleen@shirleendavies.com

Description

He'll do whatever it takes to forget the past and the woman who betrayed him.
What will he do when learning an assumed truth was a lie?

Bay's Desire, Book Nine, MacLarens of Boundary Mountain Historical Western Romance Series

Bayard Donahue lives to forget the past. The woman he loves, could never get enough of, and married, betrayed him in the worst way. The physical scars from that night don't compare to the memories he can't forget.

Suzette Gasnier shouldn't still love Bay. He abandoned her, shoving her aside without caring about the truth. Desperate to forget the man she refuses to divorce, Suzette accepts a job managing a new restaurant and hotel in Conviction, a town days away from her home in St. Louis. It's the opportunity she's dreamed of, until learning Bay is one of her bosses.

No longer interested in continuing his career as a hired gun, Bay spends his days practicing law. At night, he escorts beautiful women into the restaurant where Suzette works, making certain to flaunt them before her. He only needs her to sign the divorce decree, then he can finally put the past behind him.

At least that's what Bay thinks until learning what he thought happened in St. Louis might be far different than what he believes. And discovering someone is out to kill him.

Bay's Desire, book nine in the MacLarens of Boundary Mountain Historical Western Romance Series, is a stand-alone, full-length novel with an HEA and no cliffhanger.

Book 1: Colin's Quest
Book 2: Brodie's Gamble
Book 3: Quinn's Honor
Book 4: Sam's Legacy
Book 5: Heather's Choice
Book 6: Nate's Destiny
Book 7: Blaine's Wager
Book 8: Fletcher's Pride
Book 9: Bay's Desire

Visit my website for a list of characters for each series.
http://www.shirleendavies.com/character-list.html

Bay's Desire

Prologue

St. Louis, Missouri
1864

Bayard "Bay" Donahue worked to stay upright in his saddle, clutching the reins in one hand, the saddlehorn in the other. He hadn't incurred a gunshot wound during any of the jobs since setting aside his law degree to strap six-shooters around his hips, becoming a killer for hire.

Unlike the methodical way he approached every job in the past, he'd been careless, the desire to return to his young, beautiful wife overriding his usual caution. At least the bullet had only grazed his thigh, producing a piercing pain with no threat to his life.

Seeing the lights of St. Louis in the distance, he allowed himself to relax. But only a little. The money from the latest contract lay tucked in a small, locked pouch in his coat.

Another hour passed before he reined Spartacus, his midnight-black stallion, into the corral beside his house at the outskirts of the large, Midwestern town. Two other horses already nibbled at hay, not bothering to look up as he dismounted.

Grimacing at the throbbing pain in his leg, he slid off the bridle and removed the saddle, making short work of grooming the hungry animal. Bay glanced toward the house, gratified to see their bedroom light shining through the upstairs window.

Stepping into the kitchen, Bay removed his boots before looking down at his bloodied pants. His wife wouldn't be happy if he entered their bedroom with such a prominent wound. Instead of the lovemaking he'd been anticipating for days, he'd spend the entire night under her care. A slight smile tugged at the corners of his mouth as he slid out of the pants and doctored the torn flesh. Grabbing a folded pair of pants from a shelf in the room he often used to shed his mud-encrusted clothes, he slipped into them while inhaling the aroma of the meal she'd left on the stove.

He stopped long enough in the kitchen to finish a bowl of stew, then leaned back in the chair. For the first time, Bay wondered at the quiet in the house. It was unusual for her to hear him enter and not join him in the kitchen.

Curious, he set the empty dish in the sink and moved to the stairs. Taking them to the second floor, he stopped at the landing, hesitating when he heard nothing. No humming or movement as if she were preparing for bed. He couldn't remember a time the house had been this quiet.

Moving to the bedroom door, he stilled at the sound of a low chuckle. A man's chuckle.

Taking a step back, he placed a hand against the wall to steady himself, sucking in an unsteady breath. Bay refused to believe what he heard meant she was entertaining another man. He'd never met a more steadfast woman or devoted wife. A moment later, a deep, almost feral voice pierced through the closed door.

"You are a beauty."

Bay wondered at the lack of a response for a second before settling his hand on the doorknob. Steeling himself, he turned it, pushing slowly. His chest squeezed.

Sitting on the bed was a man wearing nothing except his pants. Standing in front of him, between his spread legs, was Bay's wife, wearing only a chemise. An almost sheer strip of material which left little to a man's imagination.

Shoving the door open all the way, he took a step inside, unable to tear his gaze from his wife's bare skin, the man's hand roaming over her.

"Get out!" His deep, guttural command reverberated around the room, drawing the attention of the stranger but not his wife. In contrast, she remained ramrod straight, her head turned away from Bay.

The man didn't move, turning his gaze on Bay. "Now, Donahue. I'd think a man such as you would have no problem sharing." He turned back to stare at her chemise covered breasts.

His hand drifting to where he'd normally find his gun, he paused. The pair of six-shooters were downstairs in the kitchen.

Taking a menacing step forward, Bay stopped several feet away, fisted hands at his sides. "Whoever you are, let go of my wife and wait for me outside."

Throwing his head back, the man laughed, tightening his grip on her hips. "So you can goad me into a gunfight, as you've done with so many others. I don't think so. All I'm after is another night with your stunning wife, and you'll not deny me the pleasure."

Hearing the incensed roar erupt from his throat, Bay lurched toward the man. An instant before he had the man's throat in his clutches, a sharp pain to his head and another to his back forced Bay to stagger. Unable to catch himself, he felt one more blow to the head before searing agony ripped through him.

Clutching his chest, Bay crumbled to the floor, hearing an animalistic scream tear from Suzette's lips an instant before the room fell into darkness.

Chapter One

Conviction, California
April 1867

Bay strolled down the boardwalk toward the newest restaurant on the town's main street, smiling at the recently installed sign. Great West Café. An enterprising young couple from San Francisco opened it the end of March, eager to capitalize on the town's booming economy.

Hidden within their meager belongings, they'd brought recipes for dishes they'd learned while working at two prestigious restaurants in the coastal city. Bay knew it had taken a good portion of their savings to install equipment and buy the six tables with four chairs each. They bought beef, chickens, and milk from the MacLarens, vegetables and fruit from neighboring farmers, and staples off the riverboats coming upriver from Sacramento.

He made it a point to come by at least three times a week for breakfast or lunch. Bay enjoyed talking to the owners, learning of their plans to expand when they had a chance. The fact everything he'd eaten was excellent didn't hurt. Besides, he appreciated people who believed in their dreams and worked hard to achieve them.

An unwelcome image of Suzette crossed his mind, a distant memory of a time when they were still in love.

Shaking his head to rid himself of the unwanted remembrance, he entered the Great West Café and took a seat. It had been almost three years, yet it still took strained effort for him to shove the pain of her betrayal aside.

Refusing to dwell on what he couldn't change, Bay smiled at Patricia Gleeson when she set down a cup filled with coffee.

"Good morning, Bay. Do you want your usual for breakfast this morning?"

He smiled. "You know me too well, Tricia. An omelet with whatever you can toss into it. How's your husband doing?"

Tricia glanced over her shoulder, then looked back at Bay with a gleam in her eyes. "Edgar's doing well. He's trying out a recipe for standing rib roast. When we worked in San Francisco, the restaurant served a fine roast, but Edgar was never happy with it. He's trying to make improvements."

Rubbing his jaw, Bay thought a moment. "I don't recall ever eating standing rib roast."

Her brows rose. "No? Well, I'll let Edgar know. He'll want me to get word to you when he's satisfied enough to offer it."

They turned when the bell on the front door chimed. The relaxed features on Bay's face froze, his stomach clenching the same as always when he saw Suzette. She stopped in the doorway, her hand still on the knob as if she planned to back out.

"Suzette." Tricia walked to her, offering a welcoming grin. "Are you here for breakfast or to talk?"

The two often spoke over coffee, comparing recipes, cooking methods, and the costs of running a restaurant. On more than one occasion, Suzette had mentioned how wonderful it would be if Tricia and Edgar ever wanted to work at the Feather River Restaurant she managed.

Suzette shot a furtive glance at Bay, shaking her head at Tricia. "Neither. I was passing by and wanted to say hello. I'll try to return tomorrow for breakfast."

"I'll make you something special, maybe sit with you for bit if there's time."

Suzette forced a smile. "I'd like that. Well, I should get back to the restaurant." Turning her back to Bay, she wrapped a hand around the knob, then glanced over her shoulder. "Perhaps we could all sit together at church on Sunday."

Tricia's face brightened. "What a lovely idea. We'll see you Sunday, if not before."

With a quick nod, Suzette left, not sparing another look at Bay.

His gaze was still locked on the closed door when Tricia came back to the table. "Would you like more coffee while I give Edgar your order?"

Swallowing, Bay nodded. "Thanks, Tricia." The good mood of several minutes before had vanished along with Suzette.

Not for the first time, Bay wondered why his law practice and business partner, August Fielder, had hired Suzette to manage the Feather River Hotel & Restaurant. Each time he asked, August would change the subject with a deft turn of a phrase or casual shrug. He knew his friend well enough to understand the older man never did anything without a reason.

She'd been in Conviction close to two years. It was well past time Bay finished what he'd started too many times to count. The divorce papers were in the safe in his office, ready for her to sign. Whenever he pulled them out, intending to meet with Suzette, something always interrupted the needed conversation.

Remaining married did nothing except cause them pain, and he was tired of living as a shadow of the man he'd once been. He wanted a real marriage with a woman who truly loved him and wanted a family. At one time, he'd thought

Suzette the perfect wife. Beautiful, witty, funny, with a huge heart and energy matching his.

He'd never thought her capable of betrayal, would've killed any man who besmirched her name or reputation. After witnessing it with his own eyes, Bay no longer saw any trace of the woman he'd fallen desperately in love with and married. All he felt was a sharp stab of pain whenever their eyes met.

Thanking Tricia when she set down his plate, he took a bite. August was leaving for Sacramento on the noon stage, due to return within a week. When he did, Bay would sit down with his partner and discover the true reason August brought Suzette to Conviction. Afterward, he'd review the divorce documents once more, meet with her, and put their relationship firmly where it belonged. In the past.

Placing a hand on her stomach to quell the anxiety seeing Bay caused, Suzette hurried away from the café. It had been close to three years since that awful night, but she still couldn't rid herself of the look of betrayal on Bay's face. She'd been over it in her head a hundred times, lying awake at night remembering what happened.

Nothing purged the horrid memory from her mind.

If he'd allowed her to explain instead of leaving St. Louis without a backward glance, everything might be different. Or maybe not. No matter the reason, Bay wasn't a man to forgive and forget. He might agree to forget a real or imagined wrong, but it never truly left his mind. Like a dog with a bone, Bay hung on, throwing past actions back at whoever slighted him. And what she'd done was no mere slight.

"Good morning, Suzette. Out for a stroll?"

A genuine smile curved her lips seeing August coming toward her. "Hello, August. It's such a nice day I decided to breathe the fresh air for a change."

He arched a brow. "Instead of the stale air in the kitchen?"

Suzette lifted one shoulder in a shrug. "Actually, yes. I've decided to either return to the kitchen and hire an assistant manager to watch the tables, or hire another cook. Either way is fine with me, but I can't work with the man we brought in from back east."

August chuckled. "Are you looking for a suggestion?"

"Absolutely."

"Let me handle getting rid of the chef. You take over as you did when we first opened the restaurant, and we'll both look for someone to work the tables in your place."

Her lips parted in surprise. "That would be wonderful, August. I miss being in the kitchen and am growing tired of supervising the servers."

"And greeting all the customers," he chuckled.

She gave a quick shake of her head. "I do enjoy meeting the diners, getting to know them. It's just..."

Taking her elbow, August guided her to a bench outside the mercantile. "Bay has been particularly hard on you lately. For that, I'm sorry. I'd thought by now his anger would've lessened enough for you to explain. I fear I was wrong about his ability to forgive enough to learn the truth."

She placed a hand on his arm. "It's not your fault. Bay's a proud man. He might never put aside his hatred for me, which means this state of tension could continue for years. I never should've accepted your offer when you traveled through St. Louis."

"Nonsense. You are the best part about the hotel and restaurant. Your skills at managing people, placating difficult guests, and offering a unique menu have made the establishment a place people all over the state travel to see. I cannot recall a better decision than the one I made bringing you to Conviction."

"But Bay's your partner. It can't be easy listening to him rage against me."

A bark of laughter passed through his lips. "Believe me, Bay isn't one to rage. He quietly simmers, which is worse in some ways. Besides, he owns twenty percent. The MacLaren family and I each own forty percent, and Ewan and Ian are very pleased with your work."

Her features softened as she thought of the two elder MacLarens. "They have been quite complimentary."

"And I see no reason for that to change. What must change is Bay. I plan to have a talk with him as soon as I return from Sacramento." Pulling out his pocket watch, August noted the time. "I must be getting to the stage station. If I miss it today, there won't be another for two days." Standing, he held out his hand to assist Suzette up. "Don't worry. This will all work out for the best." Leaning down, he kissed her cheek.

"Thank you, August. I always feel better after we talk."

Squeezing her hand, he let go. "I'm at your disposal anytime, Suzette. And don't forget. This is going to be all right. I'm absolutely certain of it."

She watched him continue down the boardwalk, wishing she held the same amount of optimism as August.

Cursing, Bay slammed the newspaper down on his desk and stood. Pacing to the window, he looked out, massaging the back of his neck, letting out a stream of curses. He didn't know who Harold Ivers, the editor of the Conviction Guardian, spoke with, but he intended to find out.

For several years, he'd been able to work and live here with few knowing his previous occupation. He'd worked hard to put the gunslinger part of his life behind him, and thought he'd been successful. Until now. In Conviction, August, Jasper Hamm, Suzette, and the MacLarens were the only ones who knew about his past, and he trusted all of them to keep his secret.

Bay stilled. Except possibly one. Suzette.

She might've been persuaded to give up the information as a way to get back at him for riding out of St. Louis, leaving her and their disaster of a marriage behind. Bay had almost turned around when he reached Kansas City. A night of gambling and drinking cured his guilt, and by morning, he'd saddled Spartacus and continued west.

Grabbing the paper, he tucked it inside his coat. August had taken the stage to Sacramento the day before. Otherwise, he might've asked his thoughts on the article, giving himself a chance to cool down before storming out to find Suzette. As it was, Bay let his anger take over.

He checked the time on the gold pocket watch Suzette had given him on their wedding day. Bay should've gotten rid of it a long time ago, but hadn't been able to bring himself to sell it.

"Ten in the morning," he mumbled, stepping outside. If he hurried, she'd still be at home. It took five minutes to navigate the already crowded boardwalk and streets before arriving at her house. Not allowing himself time to doubt his decision, he pounded on the front door and waited.

Hearing the sound of shoes on the wooden floor, he didn't wait for an invitation when Suzette drew the door open. The shock on her face might have been comical if he wasn't so angry.

She jumped aside rather than be shoved out of the way. "Bay. What in the world—"

Before she could finish, he shoved the paper in her face. "Are you the one responsible for this?"

Confusion crossed her face as she took the paper. "What do you want me to read?"

"The part about the killer for hire living in Conviction. Did you speak with Ivers?"

She read the article, shaking her head in disbelief. "No. I'd never speak to him about your past, Bay."

"Seems there are a lot of things you used to say you wouldn't do. Are you certain talking to Ivers isn't one of them?"

Shoving the paper back at him, she lifted her chin, her voice as cold as his. "What possible reason would I have for exposing your past life?"

He leaned closer. "To get back at me for abandoning you."

Throwing up her hands, she stomped from the entry into the kitchen, pulling down two cups. Without asking, she filled each with coffee, handing one to Bay. Taking a couple sips, a resolute gaze met his.

"I knew why you left. Although I wished you would've at least granted me the time to hear what happened, I understood your reasons for leaving."

"I didn't need to hear your version, Suzette. I walked in on you and the man in our bed."

She shook her head. "No. You walked in on Dave Calvan holding me *next* to the bed."

Nostrils flaring, he glared at her. "I know what I saw. What I don't know is how long you'd been allowing..." His voice faded as he let the name sink in. "Dave Calvan?"

"The man you sent to prison after you shot his brother."

Setting down the cup, he turned, pacing away. Rubbing a hand across his forehead, Bay whipped around. "It doesn't excuse the fact I caught you with him."

Shoulders sagging, she placed her cup down. "You'll always believe what you want about that night, Bay. Nothing I say will ever dissuade you from believing I cheated on you." Slipping past him into the dining room, she stopped and turned around. "I still love you. Not once have I betrayed you. Unlike you, Bay, I took our vows seriously. There's never been another man in my bed. You've always been the only one." Expelling a weary breath, she lifted a defeated gaze to meet his. "I'm tired of the pain, feeling guilty for something I had no choice about." She took a small step forward. "I know you want a divorce. I'm too tired to fight you any longer, seeing the hatred in your eyes whenever I'm close. I'll be at your office in the morning to sign the papers. Perhaps then we can both find a little peace."

Chapter Two

Cracking his eyes open, Bay dragged a hand down his face. He'd gone straight from Suzette's house back to his own, intending to work, drinking most of the day and well into the night, letting her words roll over and over in his mind.

"Not once have I betrayed you. Unlike you, Bay, I took our vows seriously."

His head pounded from drowning himself in what was left of an old bottle of whiskey, then part of a second, a gift sent to his office. He sat up on a loud groan, his stomach cramping enough to double him over for a full minute.

The morning sun already shown bright through the sheer curtain, making his eyes burn. Slowly swinging his legs off the bed, he stared at the floor, once again thinking of what Suzette said.

She'd talked to him more yesterday than in all the times they'd seen each other since that night in St. Louis. Then again, unlike all the other occasions when they might have spoken, he hadn't shunned her yesterday.

"Not once have I betrayed you."

Until now, he'd never considered what he saw and what really happened weren't the same.

"But they had to be," he muttered, pushing up to walk toward the wardrobe. Bay knew he couldn't be wrong about what he saw right in front of him. Calvan's hands rested on Suzette's nearly nude body. And she hadn't dared look at Bay, keeping her gaze averted.

That part of the horrible night had always bothered him. He'd never seen her face. Not from the time he entered the room until he awoke several days later on a cot in the clinic, Suzette asleep in a chair next to him, squeezing his hand as if she never intended to let go.

Instead of waiting for her to wake up, he'd slid his hand from hers and dressed before walking out of the clinic. He hadn't seen her again until August hired her for their new hotel and restaurant.

What if all I'd thought had been wrong?

"No." Bay ground out the word, more to clear his head than convince himself. He knew what he saw. Had never been more sure of anything in his life.

Splashing water on his face and over his head, he grabbed a towel, scrubbing harder than needed to dry his wet skin.

"Unlike you, Bay, I took our vows seriously."

This part he understood. He hadn't been discreet about the women he'd brought to Conviction via steamboat or stagecoach. He'd made certain Suzette saw every one of the stunning beauties he took to supper at the restaurant before escorting them to his house.

What Suzette didn't know was not one ever graced his bed. As much as he wanted to shove her from his heart, he'd never been able to find a woman to take her place. Never wanted anyone else to share his bed or his life. It had always been Suzette. She burned in his soul as no other woman ever had, and Bay was afraid he'd die with her still possessing his heart.

Even though she'd never believe it, he had taken their vows seriously. He also knew she hadn't been with another man, at least not since arriving in Conviction. From what August learned about her life after Bay left St. Louis, she'd taken no other lovers.

Tossing aside the towel, he dressed, a vague memory of something else Suzette said niggling at the back of his mind. Something about...

"Ah hell."

The divorce papers.

She planned to come to his office this morning to sign the papers. He'd wanted to finish this for months. Needed to put their marriage behind him and move on.

Then why had he drunk himself into a stupor when he was finally getting what he wanted? And why wasn't he hurrying to get to his office and review the papers?

The truth tore through him as surely as an arrow to the chest. Bay wasn't ready to let her go. Not after what she'd said yesterday and the doubt her words created.

Making a hasty decision, he walked downstairs and out the back door to the corral. Spartacus lifted his head, making no sound as Bay approached. Fifteen minutes later, he rode out of the gate. He needed to clear his head, think through all Suzette had said, and stay far away from her while he did both.

"Are you certain he isn't in his office, Mr. Hamm?"

Shaking his head, Jasper stood. "I'm sorry, Miss Gasnier—"

"Mrs. Donahue." Suzette cut him off in a soft voice. Inside this office, when speaking with Jasper and August, was the only time she allowed herself to be addressed as a married woman. Some days it gave her comfort. On others, it deepened the wide hole in her heart.

"Of course, Mrs. Donahue. Bay hasn't come in this morning. Are you certain he knew of the appointment?"

"We met yesterday morning about, well...there was an article in the paper, and he came by to discuss it."

Jasper had been the legal secretary for August and Bay for over two years. They depended on him to be discreet, and he'd never wavered on his job.

"Yes, I saw the article, Mrs. Donahue. Quite unfortunate. I'm certain Bay will speak to Harold Ivers and get it all straightened out. Possibly insist on a retraction. That may be where he went this morning."

Suzette had to concede Jasper might be right. Bay had been incensed at having his old life exposed in such a public way. A proud man who'd worked hard to build a new life without the stigma of being a hired gunslinger, or a wife he thought had betrayed him. At least Ivers hadn't discovered anything about Dave Calvan or the way he and his men had nearly killed Bay before leaving St. Louis. If that had come out, she wondered what Bay would've done to the newspaper editor.

"You're probably right, Mr. Hamm. I'm certain Bay had other things on his mind this morning. Please let him know I came by. He can let me know another time for the meeting. Good day."

"Good day, Mrs. Donahue." Jasper watched her leave, grimacing at the look on her face. He'd never seen a more beautiful woman with such lost and lonely eyes as his boss's wife. A woman, Jasper knew, Bay wanted to cut from his life.

It seemed so tragic. Any fool could see how much they still cared for each other. If Jasper had a woman like Suzette, he'd cherish her, never give her any reason to doubt his love and devotion. Only something terrible, an act neither could change, would've driven them so far apart.

The door opening pulled Jasper's attention from the Donahues to a man he didn't recognize.

"May I help you?"

Above average height, slim, with short brown hair and trimmed beard, Jasper guessed the man to be in his late thirties. Although the modest beard and spectacles made it hard to be certain.

"I have an appointment with Bayard Donahue. Is he in?"

Jasper ran a finger down the appointment log, seeing nothing, the same as he'd found for Suzette. "I'm sorry, but Mr. Donahue didn't list it. I'm Jasper Hamm, his assistant. You are?"

The man glanced around, ignoring the question. "Perhaps I could wait in his office."

"I apologize, but we don't allow anyone in either of the partners' offices when they aren't

22

here. I could take your name and where you're staying for Mr. Donahue when he returns."

The man continued to look around, as if memorizing each detail. Facing Jasper, his mouth twisted into a humorless grin. "The name is Jones. I'll come back another time." Reaching into his coat pocket, he removed a bottle of whiskey. "Please give this to Mr. Donahue when you see him."

Jasper cocked his head in question, taking the offered bottle before the man stepped outside, taking the boardwalk east. Dashing to the window, he watched for a moment, shrugging.

Lifting the whiskey, he studied the bottle before taking the stairs to Bay's office. "This has been an odd morning. Yes, indeed. Quite peculiar," Jasper murmured, wondering what else the day might bring.

Sheriff Brodie MacLaren strode toward the jail, the lunch his wife had prepared in one hand, the newspaper in the other. He'd read the article about Bay the night before, anger pulsing through him at the details Ivers used to expose his friend's life. It made him sick to think how many people who'd dreamed of killing Bay would show up in

Conviction, looking for either revenge or glory. Neither gave him any comfort.

"Hey, MacLaren."

Brodie whipped around, staring at the man riding toward him. Stepping from the boardwalk to the street, a smile of recognition curved his lips.

"Colt Dye." He walked toward him, waiting while Colt slid to the ground, tossing the reins over the rail. Extending his hand, they shook before Brodie slapped him on the back. "What brings you all the way from Texas to Conviction, lad?"

"My job." He followed Brodie to the door of the jail. "I've been transferred. You're looking at the new U.S. Marshal for this region."

Brodie shoved the door open, motioning for Colt to go inside. "That's grand. We need someone we can depend on. We've not had much support out here."

Taking a seat, Colt stretched out his long legs, crossing them at the ankles. "The powers in Washington finally took notice of the number of people coming this way. It doesn't hurt that San Francisco and the towns around the bay are experiencing a big increase in crime. When headquarters asked for recommendations, my captain asked if I had an interest." He shrugged, accepting the cup of coffee Brodie offered. "It was a surprise when they approved the transfer."

"I'm not surprised, lad. You're a good lawman, and you can't be bought."

Laughter preceded the door opening. Deputies Sam Covington, Seth Montero, and Alex Campbell walked in, stopping when they saw who sat across from Brodie.

"What the hell are you doing in Conviction, Colt?" Sam gripped the outstretched hand, stepping aside for Seth and Alex to do the same.

Brodie looked between his deputies. "The lad's been transferred out here."

"That's great news. We can sure use your help." Seth picked up a chair, moving it next to Colt.

"Have you already checked with your captain in San Francisco?" Alex asked, cradling a cup of coffee in his hands.

Colt nodded, his expression turning bleak. "I have." He sipped the coffee, thinking about his latest assignment and how it involved the men in this room. Draining the cup, he set it on the desk. "Appears you've got some trouble coming this way."

Brodie chuckled. "We've always got trouble, lad."

"Not like this." Colt pulled two folded papers from a pocket, sliding them across the desk to Brodie.

Opening the wanted posters, he stared at the images, read their crimes and noted the rewards before passing them to Sam. He did the same before handing them to Seth and Alex.

Brodie leaned forward, resting his arms on the desk. "Do these two men work together?"

Colt shook his head. "Not that we know about. Everett Hunt does whatever he can to avoid violence, while Andrés Delgado thrives on savagery and death."

Seth handed Brodie the posters, a brow lifting. "The Outlaw Doc?"

"Hunt is a doctor. He grew up in Georgia. Got a medical degree and was a Confederate surgeon during the war. Afterward, he made his way to the gold fields out here. From what my captain learned, he couldn't make a go of it and tried gambling. Hunt couldn't make a living at that, either."

Sam rubbed his jaw. "So he became a highwayman."

Colt nodded. "He goes by Ev Hunt, but the reporters call him the Outlaw Doc. I guess it sells more newspapers." His mouth twisted in disgust. "I heard there are dime novels written about him. He prefers to work alone, but does sometimes bring in others. They target lone riders, stages, and wagons moving ore from the mines."

"Is he successful at not hurting his victims?" Alex asked.

Colt shrugged. "Mostly."

Seth narrowed his gaze. "Mostly?"

"He *will* kill if those he robs don't cooperate or if they pull a weapon. Once in a while, he does a job for someone else."

Brodie tilted his head. "Such as?"

"Similar to a gun for hire, except Hunt doesn't complete the contract with a gun. Because of his medical knowledge, he uses other methods."

Sam nodded. "Methods that would be harder to track."

Colt's mouth twisted. "He's highly intelligent. Believes he can get away with most anything. So far, he has."

Standing, Seth walked to the stove, refilling his cup. "What about Andrés Delgado?"

"He's a little more of a mystery. Delgado prefers going after lone travelers, especially those coming off a winning streak in the saloons. The man has no problem killing or maiming, and that includes women."

"Children?" Brodie asked.

"Not that I've heard. People don't turn him in because he has a habit of sharing his take with those in need. He's been quoted as saying *'Take from the rich and give to the poor.'* My captain says Delgado sees himself as the man in the legend."

Brodie chuckled. "Aye. Ma used to tell us stories of Robin Hood. Colin, Quinn, Blaine, and the other lads couldn't get enough." Sobering, he fixed his gaze on Colt. "You're thinking Delgado is in the area?"

Colt nodded. "Makes sense. He has a sister in Conviction."

Brodie arched a brow. "Ach. You could've started with that information, lad." Standing, he walked around the desk to rest a hip against the edge. "Who's his sister?"

Colt smirked. "Maria Smith."

Brodie glanced at the others, seeing no sign of recognition. "Are you sure she lives here?"

"Or close by. Do you know of any Smiths in the area?" Colt asked.

Sam stood, stretching his arms above his head. "There's a passel of Smiths all through the gold region. Men doing their best to get away from their families, outlaws trying to hide. I'd guess there must be a couple hundred between Sacramento and Settlers Valley. I don't know how many live around Conviction."

Colt looked at Brodie. "We need to identify all those within ten miles."

Alex picked up the posters, scanning them once more. "Why is locating the sister so important?"

Pushing up from his chair, Colt pursed his lips. "Because Delgado and his sister are close. If anyone gets any of his take, it's her. And he always delivers the money in person."

Chapter Three

Bay swung down from Spartacus, placing a hand on the saddle to steady himself as he hit the ground. He grimaced as waves of nausea doubled him over. Never had he experienced such disagreeable effects after imbibing in too much whiskey. Not even during the days following Suzette's betrayal when he'd almost lived on the amber liquid.

Straightening, he rubbed his temples to relieve the relentless pounding. It had plagued him since waking that morning and showed no sign of subsiding.

Bay hadn't planned to be gone most of the day when he rode out of the corral. All he wanted was an hour or two to clear his head, making certain Suzette couldn't find him if she did intend to sign the papers.

A wry chuckle burst from his lips. She'd offered what he'd wanted for a long time, yet instead of staying in town, obtaining her signature, he'd chosen to put distance between them.

Bay didn't understand his actions and had no intention of taking time today to figure them out. Not with his brain functioning at the pace of thick molasses, his stomach roiling like the Pacific

Ocean. It had been years since her actions had torn them apart. A few more days or weeks wouldn't make any difference.

He stared at the land before him. The MacLaren ranch, Circle M, stretched for miles in all directions. Their property touched the Feather River in places, but they'd never expanded across the water's edge. He'd always wondered why, never feeling the urge to ask his friends.

Instead, they'd purchased a vast amount of land to the north, which included several existing ranches. Blaine MacLaren had been selected as foreman of the property near Settlers Valley, along with help from Heather MacLaren Stewart and her husband, Caleb. A few months ago, Heather and Caleb became the parents of a baby boy, Joshua.

Bay's jaw clenched at the thought of how many MacLarens near his age were marrying, having children. He and Suzette had often spoken of starting a family, deciding to wait until he hung up his guns for good.

She wanted at least three children. Bay had always told her he'd be happy to oblige. They'd laughed about his eagerness to please her, which she'd always responded to by saying he was just eager to find his own pleasure. Bay had never denied it. Suzette had given him incredible pleasure, in every sense of the word. More than he'd ever expected or deserved.

Leaning down, Bay pulled a stem of sourgrass from the ground, chewing on the bright yellow flowers. A somewhat bitter taste filled his mouth as he walked along the top of the hill, his thoughts still on Suzette and the life they'd once shared.

Again, her words popped into his head. *"Not once have I betrayed you."* Six words that took hold, clawing at his memory of the night he'd walked in on her and Calvan.

Tossing the sourgrass aside, he massaged the back of his neck, his mind in turmoil. He no longer knew what to believe. Nor could he clearly recall the haunting vision which had plagued him for years. Those six words had torn through him, making him doubt himself and what he'd seen. Or thought he'd seen.

"But I *did* see it," he ground out as a fresh wave of frustration gripped his chest.

Unable to think over the pounding in his head, he swung into the saddle. Reining Spartacus toward town, Bay took the trail back at a slow pace, not quite ready to return to his office or the beautiful house he'd built next door to August.

For all the fancy fixtures and expensive furnishings, it had never filled his need for a true home. A place he looked forward to returning to each night. Instead, it had become a large wooden tomb where he slept and sometimes ate. It had never become a home, and he had serious doubts it ever would be.

Suzette couldn't keep herself from watching the front door of the restaurant. She alternated between wanting to see Bay and hoping he wouldn't show for supper as he did most nights. Their discussion a few days before hadn't gone well, leaving her with an intense sense of defeat.

He hated her. The thought caused a familiar ball of ice to form in her stomach. She'd hoped at some point, after enough time had passed, he'd listen to her side. Their heated discussion revealed he never intended to hear her out. The realization cut deep, dashing all her hopes for finding a reconciliation someday. She now knew whatever they'd once had was over.

Suzette had gone by his office each day since they'd argued, but he'd been otherwise occupied or gone. This morning, exasperated and ready to accept the futility of hoping their marriage could be saved, she'd asked Jasper to request Bay give him the papers. Tomorrow, she'd steel her resolve, return to his office, and end the pain of the last few years.

Hearing the door open, laughter coming from those who entered, Suzette turned to see Bay walk in with one more in an ongoing stream of beautiful women. Each time it felt as if he'd plunged a knife into her chest. Rather than moving toward them, she turned to one of the servers.

"Please seat Mr. Donahue and his guest."

The young man didn't hide his surprise. It had become common practice for Suzette to seat Bay, August, and the MacLarens. All owned a percentage of the hotel and restaurant, and all were her bosses.

"Are you sure, ma'am?"

Suzette shot him a bemused look before turning toward the kitchen. "Completely." She didn't glance into the dining room, already knowing how Bay would react.

Hiding in the kitchen wouldn't accomplish anything except time to deal with the anger. Of course he found time to escort another stunning woman around Conviction when he couldn't spare ten minutes for her.

"Miss Gasnier?" The young server came through the door, concern etched on his face.

"Yes?"

He licked his lips, glancing at the kitchen staff, then back at her. "Mr. Donahue insists you attend to his needs."

Anger flared at the obvious intent to humiliate her. "Attend to his needs?"

Looking down at the floor, he nodded. "Yes, ma'am. He and his guest refuse to take a table unless you seat them."

She gripped her hands in front of her, fighting the urge to storm into the dining room and tell him to go to hell. If only August had returned from Sacramento. He wouldn't allow Bay to treat her this way. August would be gracious, a concept Bay had never embraced.

The young man shuffled from one foot to the other. "What should I tell him?"

Knowing she had no choice, Suzette accepted defeat. "I'll *attend* to him."

Leaving the kitchen, she stiffened her spine, forcing a smile as she strolled slowly around tables to the front door. Approaching them, Suzette looked between the two, her resolve slipping.

The woman was stunning. Sleek black hair coiled into an intricate chignon, finished with a gold clip adorned with pearls. The royal blue gown fit her curves to perfection, even if it did seem a little out of place in Conviction. Her ivory complexion complemented oval, chocolate brown eyes, which were locked on Bay's face. Suzette tried to ignore the way her arm was tucked through his in an obvious possessive gesture. The thought of them together sickened her, as it had with every woman he'd flaunted. As always, Suzette ignored the twisting in her gut, the stab to her heart.

"Good evening, Mr. Donahue. Apologies for not being here to greet you immediately, but there was a slight, well...problem in the kitchen." Her sugary voice wasn't lost on Bay, who didn't hide his irritation. "If you'll please follow me." She stopped at his usual table. "Here you are."

Suzette waited as Bay pulled out a chair for his guest, then made a decision she knew wouldn't bode well for her future at the restaurant. Looking at the woman, she cocked her head, as if studying her.

"I thought I knew all of Bay's women, but I don't believe we've met." Suzette smiled sweetly. "I'm Suzette Donahue. And you are?"

The woman gasped, her gaze shifting between Bay and Suzette. "Donahue? Are you two related?"

Suzette looked at him. "Don't tell me you haven't told your latest paramour of our relationship, Bay."

The woman's face flushed, eyes flashing. She glared at Bay. "Paramour?"

"I see my husband didn't tell you he's married. He often does forget such trivialities." Glancing at Bay, Suzette felt a rush of satisfaction at the way his nostrils flared and jaw clenched. "Would you care for wine?"

"Excuse me." The woman stood, her hostile gaze directed at Bay. "I'll find my supper somewhere else tonight, *Mr. Donahue*." She stormed away, not waiting for his response.

Bursting to his feet, Bay took Suzette's arm, guiding her away from the other diners before rounding on her. "What the hell are you doing?"

Refusing to cower, she pulled her arm free. "Only stating the truth, which is what I should've done the first time you brought one of your lovers in here." Crossing her arms, she scowled at him. "I've decided to no longer hide the fact we're married, Bay. If you don't like it, finalize the divorce and get me out of your life." She waited a moment before stomping toward the dining room.

"Suzette," he ground out.

She didn't respond, lifting a hand in dismissal.

Bay stared after her, simultaneously angry and fascinated by her bold move. For the first time since he'd left her, he saw the feisty woman he'd fallen in love with years before. Eyes flashing, daring him to challenge her, Bay couldn't help the fierce attraction rushing through him.

Standing there, still stunned by what she'd done, a smile curved the corners of his mouth. She'd never dared to defy him before, never publicly exposed their relationship. He wondered how many others overheard her announcement. Instead of embarrassment, pride and desire gripped him. He wanted his wife now as much as when they'd met.

The thought confused him. Bay had never truly hated her for what happened, but he'd never been able to forgive her for cuckolding him, either. No man would.

Still, the way Suzette insisted she'd never betrayed him, then announced their true relationship tonight astounded him. Before the incident with Calvan, he'd witnessed this type of audacious behavior from her numerous times. Since coming to Conviction, she'd been meek, soft-spoken, recoiling from him. She'd never mentioned the women he'd paraded through town before tonight.

An odd rush of guilt seized him. He'd sought revenge by humiliating her for the way she'd betrayed him. Although he'd never taken a single one of the women to bed, Suzette didn't know that, which was what he wanted. Causing her pain gave him a measure of satisfaction. At least it had before their argument a few days ago and her outburst tonight.

Something didn't make sense. Suzette had never been able to lie to him. When she insisted she'd never betrayed him, he wanted to believe her, but couldn't reconcile what he'd seen from her adamant denial.

Now she refused to pretend their marriage didn't exist. Her actions were unexpected, and Bay had no idea what to think of the change.

He couldn't dwell on the shift in her behavior now, not with the woman he'd brought from Sacramento wandering the streets. Bay would find her and apologize. After he made certain she'd eaten, he'd secure a room for her in the Gold Dust Hotel. Tomorrow, he'd put her on the steamship south.

Afterward, he'd lock himself in his office and decide what to do about Suzette, their marriage, and the raging desire he could no longer ignore.

Andrés Delgado pulled out a cheroot, reaching down to strike a lucifer against the heel of his boot. Lighting the slim cigar, he leaned back against the fallen log, watching the fire as well as the town in the distance.

He'd planned to continue to Maria's home tonight, give her money, and leave before anyone spotted him. That was before he'd sent one of his two men into Conviction. What the man said upon returning forced Andrés to rethink riding directly to his sister's.

Brodie MacLaren and his deputies were searching for a family named Smith. Specifically Maria Delgado Smith. He felt confident they wouldn't find her. Not with the land titled under another name, a distant relative living in New Mexico with no outward connection to the Delgados.

Taking a long draw from the cheroot, Andrés closed his eyes, deciding his next move. Maria needed the money. Not so much for food, as she raised a few head of cattle and always had several dozen chickens running about. She also tended a large garden and had two dairy cows. The money was for supplies and feed, fabric for sewing clothes for herself and the children, and for running if necessary. Andrés had no intention of letting the last happen.

He understood them coming after him. After all, Andrés had committed terrible crimes in his life, most rivaling those of any other outlaw wandering the western territory. Murder, robbery, torture, even rape. Never once had he felt guilty for what he'd done. Maria believed he had no heart, no soul when it came to most people. She and her children were the exception.

Andrés would do everything he could to protect them. Hadn't he taken care of her abusive husband? He'd provided her property, money, and his protection. In his mind, it would never be enough to repay his sister for the beatings she'd taken to keep their depraved father away from him. She'd been older, stronger, accepting all their father's cruelty when they were younger. Scars covered her body. Once, he'd beaten her so badly she'd lost hearing in one ear and much of the sight in an eye. All to protect her younger brother.

When he'd turned fifteen, everything changed. As if overnight, Andrés grew several inches, surpassing his father in both height and weight. It had taken only one beating from him to send his father riding away. He'd never returned, and they'd never missed him. From that day on, Andrés had become Maria's protector. Or, as she would say in her soft voice, her savior.

No one, not Brodie MacLaren or any other lawman, would threaten the sister who Andrés' unwavering love. But he'd heard stories about the sheriff and his deputies. They never gave up, always hunting until they found their prey. He knew it wouldn't be long before they discovered her location.

She'd tell them nothing, of that he felt certain. Unless they threatened the children. Andrés didn't know if MacLaren was like so many other lawmen, thinking it their right to intimidate women and children to find what they sought. He might not be, but Andrés couldn't take the chance.

Tossing the stub of the cheroot into the dirt, he looked at his two men, the only people he trusted besides Maria.

"Tomorrow, we ride to my sister's, give her the money, and find a place to camp." A feral smile broke across his face. "Then we wait for MacLaren and his men."

Chapter Four

Bay shoved the covers away, cursing under his breath. He hadn't had that much whiskey the night before, yet again, his head felt as if it would explode. Standing, he bent over, groaning at the intense stomach cramps.

Waiting until the pain faded, he straightened, staring at his hands. Both tingled. Not a lot, but enough so he noticed. Shaking them, he felt a wave of relief when the tingling sensations stopped. After all these years of enjoying whiskey, Bay didn't understand why a couple drinks would send his body lurching.

Going to the dresser, he splashed water on his face and neck, then dressed, all the while thinking of Suzette. He hadn't seen her since the night in the restaurant when she'd introduced herself as his wife.

At first, he'd been angry, furious at how she'd driven away the woman who'd traveled all the way from Sacramento to spend time with him. A woman he had no intention of bedding or seeing again.

Thinking about that night, a wry grin appeared, remembering how Suzette had turned things back on him. She'd stood up for herself, the same as she had when they'd argued, asserting she'd never betrayed him.

What bothered him was her true reason for speaking out. She'd done it to push him into finalizing their divorce. Even through her bravado, he'd seen the hurt on her face when he'd walked into the restaurant with another woman. The same pain he'd seen her try to conceal each time he'd appeared with a stunning beauty on his arm.

The satisfaction he used to experience at Suzette's distressed reaction had changed to guilt over the last few weeks. Bay wondered why he continued to bring women to Conviction when they meant nothing to him. After everything, the only woman he wanted was his wife.

He strapped on his gunbelt and grabbed his hat. August would be back from Sacramento on the morning steamship and Bay planned to waylay him for a meeting. The time had come for his mentor to explain his real reason for bringing Suzette to Conviction.

As competent a manager as she was, he knew there had to be more behind August's paying for her passage from St. Louis when someone from San Francisco could've been hired. Bay already suspected the reason, but needed August to confirm it.

Stopping for a quick breakfast at the Great West Café, he read the latest edition of the Guardian. He and Harold Ivers had a long, heated conversation after the editor ran the story of Bay's past life, finally coming to an understanding.

On this week's second page was a clarification of the original story, but not the full retraction Bay sought. For now, he'd let it go. If Ivers wrote any more about him, there would be hell to pay.

"Here you are." Tricia set down a plate of eggs, bacon, and a crêpe with wild berry compote. "You're the first customer to try this."

Bay stared at the dessert-like concoction, tilting his head. "Well, I'm willing to give it a try if I can also get some of your bread."

Laughing, Tricia headed back to the kitchen, returning a few minutes later with thick slices of sourdough slathered with butter. "Let me know if you need more."

Bay tucked into his breakfast, meaning to make it a quick meal before walking to the docks to meet August. Hearing the chime over the door, he glanced up, his features stilling. Suzette stood in the doorway. He could see the indecision on her face when she spotted him.

"Don't rush off because of me, Suzette. In fact, why don't you join me? I'll let you try some of this new concoction Tricia put on my plate." He nodded at the crêpe.

Hesitating a moment, she walked to his table, her face guarded. Then she glanced down at the plate. "Oh, a berry crêpe. I wondered when she and Edgar would put them on the menu."

Standing, Bay pulled out a chair. "Please sit down. I promise not to cause a scene."

Biting her lower lip, Suzette studied his face. "Why? Did you bring the papers you want me to sign?"

"No, I didn't." Frustration tinged his words. "I'll understand if you'd prefer to eat alone."

Feeling a little foolish at making such a fuss over a simple request, she nodded. "All right."

Once she sat down, he returned to his seat. Pushing the plate toward her, Bay pointed to the crêpe. "I'd appreciate it if you'd try this first."

She cocked a brow, her lips twitching. "Do you think it's poisoned?"

He didn't return her lightheartedness. "If I did, I wouldn't be offering you any."

Ignoring the strange tone in his voice, she let her fork hover over the crêpe. "I'd think that would be agreeable to you. After all, it would put an end to all the trouble between us." Sliding a portion onto her fork, she placed it into her mouth, missing the flash of unease on Bay's face. "Oh, this is wonderful. You must have some."

"Do you think it's too sweet for me?"

Chuckling, she shook her head. "No. It isn't any sweeter than the berry pie you like so much. Really, I do believe you'd like it."

Tricia walked up with another full plate of eggs, bacon, and another crêpe. "I decided to serve you the same as Bay. I hope it's all right."

Suzette looked up, grinning. "This is fine, Tricia. The crêpe is marvelous. Will you be putting it on the menu?"

"Edgar plans to. He wanted to get some comments before making a final decision. So, what do you think of it, Bay?"

He scooped up some on his fork, taking a quick glance at Suzette before placing it into his mouth. A moment later, he looked between the two women. "This is very good, Tricia. Excellent, in fact."

Sending a knowing grin at Suzette, she smiled. "Wonderful. I'll let Edgar know." She headed for the kitchen, leaving them alone.

They ate in silence for several minutes before Bay set down his fork, picking up the cup of coffee. "I'll be meeting August at the docks after breakfast. Would you care to accompany me?"

The offer came as such a surprise, she dropped her fork, feeling her face flush. "I, um...that would be lovely."

"Good." He continued eating, saying nothing more until they'd both cleaned their plates. When

Tricia told them the price for each meal, he pulled out enough for both, then stood.

"I can pay for my own breakfast, Bay."

"I'm certain you can, Suzette." Holding out a hand, he assisted her up. "Don't let the fact I paid for your meal ruin your day." Although his expression stayed somber, his lips curved up enough for her to know his words were in jest.

Stepping outside, he took her hand, slipping it through his arm while ignoring the way her body tensed. They walked a short distance before Suzette glanced at him.

"What are you doing, Bay?"

"Escorting you to the docks to meet August."

"What I mean is, why are you being so nice to me? You've not said a civil word to me since..." Her voice trailed off, not wanting to bring up the worst night of her life.

"Since you decided to choose Calvan over me?"

Stopping, she pulled her arm free. Looking around to make certain no one watched, she leaned toward him. "I *never* chose him over you, and I'm tired of enduring your scorn day after day." She took a step closer, a finger poking him in the chest, her voice hard and unyielding. "I'll be at your office this afternoon to end our marriage. I expect you to be there." Turning away, she stopped to glance over her shoulder. "Don't do what you always do, Bay."

Controlling his anger, he glared at her. "And what is that?"

"Show your cowardice and run."

An hour later, Bay still seethed as he sat across the desk from August in his partner's office.

He'd met the steamboat, impatient when it took longer than expected for the older man to disembark. Once on land, Bay took August aside. "We need to talk."

As if he understood the need in Bay's voice, he nodded, not asking any questions until they'd shut the door of his office and taken seats. Resting his arms on his desk, August studied the younger man who'd become as close as a son.

"What is it you want to discuss?"

"Suzette."

Brow quirking up, a knowing grin lifted the corners of his mouth. "I wondered when you'd decide to ask about her."

Bay tilted his head, gaze narrowing.

"It took you longer than I expected." August chuckled, eliciting a surprised look from Bay. "So, what is it you want to know?"

A little disconcerted by August's comments, Bay leaned back in his chair, so many questions rolling through his head. He decided to ask the most important one. "Why did you bring her here?"

"Because Suzette filled every requirement we had for the manager of our hotel and restaurant."

"I know there's more. Why else?"

Shrugging, August's features sobered. "She's your wife, Bay. Not that you don't already know your relationship with the lovely woman."

"Our relationship isn't important."

"It's *all* that's important. I know you well enough to know you'd never have married Suzette if you didn't love her. What I don't understand is why you rode off, leaving her alone and unprotected. I had no idea of the relationship between the two of you until I mentioned your name as one of my business partners. It took long hours of convincing before she agreed to give up her job and travel to Conviction." The disappointment in August's voice drew a grimace from Bay. "Tell me why you left her."

Swallowing the bile he always fought whenever he remembered the night he'd found her with Calvan, he pushed aside the pain to meet August's hard gaze.

"I found her with another man."

"Are you sure about that, Bay?" He held up a hand when Bay opened his mouth to reply. "Think carefully on this before you answer. Sometimes what we *think* we see isn't reality. Over time, it becomes our reality, even when it's false."

Jumping up, Bay paced to the window, then whipped around to face August. His features hardened, voice accusing. "What do you know of what happened?"

Relaxing, he sat back in his chair, unmoved by Bay's undisguised anger. "There's a good deal you don't know about what happened that night. Perhaps if you'd stayed in St. Louis after regaining consciousness, you'd be enjoying a much different life than the one you have now."

Bay's hand speared through his thick, dark hair as he took a step toward August. "What the hell are you trying to tell me?"

"I'm not the one you should be asking. You're going to have to ask Suzette, and I hope you'll listen with an open mind."

Chest heaving in anger, Bay lowered himself back into the chair. "How do you know what she'd tell me will be the truth?"

"Because after I heard Suzette's story, I spoke to the doctor who tended you, the sheriff, and one of the men who rode with Dave Calvan. If you'd been more interested in discovering the truth, you wouldn't be asking what you should already know." Standing, August walked around his desk, resting a hip against the edge and folding his arms over his chest. His gaze locked on Bay's, waiting.

After a few long moments, Bay scrubbed a hand down his face. "Suzette is coming to the office this afternoon to end our marriage."

"Good."

Bay's eyes widened. "Good?"

"Yes. It will give you the opportunity to ask the questions you should've asked years ago. Afterward, you can decide if you're willing to do whatever is needed to convince her to give you another chance."

His voice was incredulous. "Give *her* another chance? Suzette is the one who broke our vows."

August lifted a brow. "Are you certain?"

Bay paused, admitting to himself he did have doubts. Intense ones which had vexed him for days. Meeting August's gaze, he didn't respond.

"I thought so." Pushing away from the desk, August walked to his office door, opening it. "I'd suggest you start preparing for your meeting with Suzette and the questions you intend to ask." He held the door wide as Bay stood, walking toward him. "You're doing what's right."

Anger beginning to fade, he gave August a weary look. "I hope you're right."

Chapter Five

Suzette stared into the mirror, building her courage before leaving for Bay's office. Taking extra time to prepare herself had become a common routine whenever she expected to see him, which meant every day since he often took at least one meal at the Feather River Restaurant.

Today's ritual felt different, giving Suzette hope the decision she'd made was right. Month after long month of tolerating his scorn and enduring the pain as he brought one woman after another into the restaurant had broken her spirit, forced her to fight each day for the tiniest scrap of dignity. She'd reached her limit.

Divorce was uncommon, seen as a blemish on both parties, but more so on the woman. In fact, Suzette hadn't heard of a single one being submitted in Conviction.

Nevertheless, she no longer cared about societal restraints or what others might think of her. She felt confident her few friends, mainly the MacLarens, would understand. Dissolving her marriage to Bay would provide a clear future, a chance to find love a second time and start the family she'd dreamed about.

Breathing in a last, fortifying breath, she turned toward the door, knowing the time had come to meet with Bay. Securing a hat atop her head, she picked up her reticule and left.

Taking her time, she lifted her face to the sun, loving the feel of the warm rays kissing her skin. Suzette didn't rush the journey from one side of town to the other. With the decision made, she no longer felt the need to hurry. She was giving her husband what he wanted, allowing herself the ability to forget and move on.

Nodding at several people she recognized, Suzette made the last turn onto the main street. She glanced inside the mercantile, barber shop, gunsmith, and the Merchant Bank as she passed, slowing her pace, then stopping. Walking through the doorway would take her to Bay and the end of her current life.

A sharp pain clutched at her chest. Pressing a hand against it, she tried to breathe, finding it almost impossible.

"You can do this, Suzette." She'd chanted the phrase several times before saying it out loud as she gripped the doorknob. "You *must* do this."

Straightening, she lifted her chin and entered. Jasper's greeting came before she'd closed the door.

"Good afternoon, Miss...I mean, Mrs. Donahue. Mr. Donahue said you might be coming in for a meeting." He stood, walking to the bottom of the stairs, gesturing upward. "He's waiting for you in his office."

She nodded, offering a weak smile. "Thank you, Jasper."

Memories of their life together flashed across her mind with each tread. Sharing their pasts, teasing each other, her laughing at Bay's antics, him smiling just before he'd lean down to kiss her. Stopping at the landing, she pressed a hand to her chest once more. Suzette forced herself to recall the reasons their marriage had to end.

Taking the remaining stairs on laden feet, she took the final step, moving to his office. She jumped when the door opened, startling her. Bay stood a couple feet away, a broad grin enhancing his already handsome face. She briefly wondered about his bright smile before her spirits fell. He wanted this over as much as she did.

"Good afternoon, Suzette."

She glanced at him, her face neutral. "Bay."

"Please, come in." After she entered, he closed the door and pulled out a chair at a small table. "It will be more comfortable to talk here rather than across my desk." Grabbing papers and a fountain pen from his desk, he took a seat next to her, his thigh touching hers. Feeling her flinch away, he chuckled. "I won't bite, you know." That was when he saw the deep sadness in her eyes, the pain she always tried to hide. He grimaced, recalling how his anger had pushed him to humiliate and ridicule her, often in front others.

"Can we please get this over with?"

Hearing the broken determination in her voice, he cringed. He dropped the papers and pen on the table, leaning back in his chair to study her face, settling on the emerald green eyes which had drawn him since the first day he'd spotted her in St. Louis. Letting his gaze wander over her porcelain skin, a slow grin tilted the corners of his mouth seeing the sprinkling of freckles across her nose and cheeks. Then he allowed himself a moment to focus on her lips. Full and luscious. The kind which weakened any man.

"Bay?"

Her voice pulled him back to the reason for the meeting. This time when his gaze met hers, he saw the intense strain in her eyes, the new lines of worry, her pinched lips. Then he remembered August telling him to ask questions and listen to her answers without recriminations.

Shifting his attention to the papers, he touched them. "These are the papers that will end our marriage. Well, after the circuit judge comes through and approves them."

"All right. Would you let me know where to sign?" She reached out, meaning to pick up the pen. Before she could, he swept the papers and pen to the far side of the table. Her brows drew together. "What are you doing?"

Glancing away, he let out a harsh breath, unsure of what drove him to stall her efforts to sign the documents ending their marriage. Resting his arms on the table, he cocked his head.

"I have questions, and I believe you have the answers, Suzette." He saw her bottom lip tremble before she lifted her chin.

"Questions about what?"

"The night I found you with Calvan."

Clasping her hands in her lap, she tilted her head. "Isn't it a little late for you to ask?"

"It's never too late to learn the truth."

Pursing her lips, she wondered if it would be best to come back another time, knowing it was a foolish notion. She shrugged. "I doubt anything you hear from me will change your mind. What you saw is what you believe."

Reaching out, he placed a hand over hers. He almost jerked it away, feeling the biting chill of her skin. "You're freezing." Standing, he lifted his coat jacket from its hook. "Here." He draped it over her shoulders before returning to his chair. "Better?"

Suzette nodded, although she hadn't noticed the chill. She *could* feel the tremors rippling through her body, the tightness in her chest, the shaking of her hands.

"Yes. Thank you."

"Do you want coffee or tea? Jasper can have it up here within minutes."

She shook her head. "No. The coat is fine."

"Is it all right to ask my questions?"

Rubbing her temples, she bit her lower lip. "I don't know what you expect, Bay. You've never been interested before." She wondered for an instant if she should tell him the worst part about talking of that night. "It's hard to talk about it." Pressing a hand against her stomach, she tried to control the shakes, which always came when she remembered the worst night of her life. "I can't..."

Getting up again, he walked to a cabinet, taking out a bottle of whiskey and two glasses. Pouring a portion into each, he returned to the table, holding one out to her.

"Drink this. It'll help calm you."

Taking it from him, she took one sip, then another before setting the glass down. She'd always preferred to drink Bay's favorite liquor, never learning to enjoy sherry as many of the women who came into the restaurant favored.

Lowering himself into the chair, he took a small swallow, watching as Suzette's hands began to still. "Better?"

Finishing the last sip, she licked her lips, nodding. She had no idea what the small gesture did to Bay. The way his body tightened watching the slow way her tongue drew across her glorious lips.

Bay shifted in his chair, clearing his throat. "Can we talk about—"

She held up her hand, interrupting what he planned to say. "Why now, Bay? I've asked, almost begged you several times to let me explain, but you've always walked away. You've never shown the slightest interest in hearing my side." Her voice had risen with each sentence, the accusatory tone clear, making him flinch.

"Maybe I think it's time." He grimaced at how ridiculous the excuse sounded.

Staring at him, her gaze narrowed. "Well, maybe I think it's too late."

Standing, Suzette marched to the cabinet, taking out the bottle. Returning to the table, she added a little to his glass and filled her own, setting the bottle on the table. Sitting down, she took a slow sip, glancing at him over the rim of the glass.

"Nothing's been decided, Suzette. If you explain—"

"You don't understand." She gripped her hands in her lap, exhaling a slow breath.

"What don't I understand?"

Her face twisted in pain. "You've spent almost two years humiliating me with your numerous women. There isn't anyone in this town who would believe we are married. Why would they? They see you as a hardworking single man, taking your pleasure whenever and with whomever you choose." Her voice broke on the last. She shoved his hand away when he reached toward her. "Even if you believe my side of what happened, I'll never live down the shame of being the woman whose husband purposely cast her aside." Letting out a broken sob of distress, she swiped away moisture in her eyes. Jumping up, she grabbed her reticule. "I need to leave."

Beating her to the door, he blocked her escape. "Don't leave, Suzette."

Her gaze darted around the room as if looking for a way out before glaring at him. "I have to leave. *Now.*"

This time, she couldn't stop the tears from falling. Spinning away, she scrubbed both hands down her face, doing what she could to regain her composure. Feeling Bay's hands on her shoulders, she flinched away. Taking several deep breaths, she turned around, surprised at the stricken look on Bay's face.

"Please. Just let me go." Her words meant more than allowing her to leave his office.

Refusing to step aside, he shook his head. "I can't."

Taking a step closer, anger building, she placed her palms on his chest, shoving hard. "Get out of my way."

He shook his head, unable to cause her more pain. "All right." He walked back to the table and picked up the papers. Holding them in front of him, he tore the documents down the middle.

Her eyes widened, hands balled into fists at her sides. "What are you doing?"

Setting the torn pages aside, he walked to her, settling his hands on her shoulders. "I won't sign anything until I understand that night."

"Then I'll sign them."

He shook his head. "I'm afraid that won't work. For you to get a divorce without my consent, you need to prove adultery, abandonment, cruelty, or desertion."

"It won't be hard. You have committed adultery and abandoned me."

"And how will you prove either?"

She threw back her head, staring at the ceiling. "It's no secret you've brought women into town, welcoming them into your bed. We live in different houses. A married couple wouldn't do such a thing."

His features softened, one corner of his mouth curving upward. "Any of the women will tell you how they spent the night in a separate bedroom." He felt no satisfaction at the way her face twisted in confusion, then denial.

"That can't be true."

His voice lowered. "It's quite true."

"But why?" Even as she spoke the words, Suzette realized the truth. "You *planned* to hurt me. Make me pay for what you thought I'd done to you." She twisted out of his hold, taking a step away. "You were cruel and vile." Her breath came in short gasps, understanding the depth of his retribution.

He jerked as if she'd slapped him. "I deserve your anger at what I did."

"Then you know why I want the divorce. I could *never* love a man who took such enjoyment at seeing me broken." Bile rose in her throat. She never believed she could hate Bay. She'd been wrong. "I can charge you with abandonment or desertion."

He let out a regretful breath. "I'm afraid that won't work, either. August will admit you insisted on your own house when you came to Conviction."

"I never..." Her voice trailed off when she remembered her discussion with August about living arrangements. He suggested she stay at Bay's so they could try to work out their differences. She'd adamantly refused.

"There is a way to settle this, Suzette." His voice was soft, conciliatory.

She shook her head, looking up to meet his gaze. "How?"

"You tell me what happened. Once I understand, we'll put it behind us and continue our married life."

Her eyes flashed, eyes bulging. "Are you mad? After all you've done to me, I'll never live with you again. Never!"

Chapter Six

Suzette performed her duties at the restaurant as if nothing had happened in Bay's office. Her clothes, hair, and composure would lead no one to suspect the tumultuous meeting, which had left her confused and exhausted.

She wondered how he could even imagine a future after the way he'd humiliated her in the most public way. Anyone who knew either of them would be appalled to learn they were wed yet didn't acknowledge their union. It would be worse due to his behavior of bedding other women, becoming an adulterer.

After stating he hadn't bedded any of them, she no longer knew what to believe. Suzette did know whatever had happened in the privacy of his home between him and the women he flaunted before her, he'd meant to cause a great deal of suffering. It had worked beautifully.

Suzette couldn't count the nights she'd sought sleep, tears streaming down her cheeks, picturing Bay a few houses away making love to someone else. There had been times the pain had been so intense she felt physically ill. At some point, sleep always came, the hurt subsiding enough for her to face another day.

"Miss Gasnier, there is a gentleman at the door asking for you. I told him we're about ready to close for the evening, but he insisted."

She nodded at the young server. "Thank you."

Smoothing her hands down the long, black skirt, she straightened, a disingenuous smile forming on her face. Expecting Bay, she took her time moving between the few tables still occupied at this hour. Approaching the front, she lifted her gaze, a sincere smile brightening her face.

"Griff." Holding out her hands, she grasped both of his.

"Hello, Suzette." Griffin MacKenzie leaned down, brushing a quick kiss across her cheek.

"It's been too long." She looked across the almost deserted room, pleased to see a table in the darkened alcove empty. "I'll show you to a table."

"Are you able to join me?"

She glanced around. "I'd love to. Let me talk to one of the servers." Returning a moment later, Suzette sat in the chair Griff pulled out, pleased he'd asked. It had been a while since she'd relaxed over a late supper with a friend.

"It's good to see you, Suz."

She smiled at the nickname Griff gave her years ago, a time when their lives hadn't been burdened as they were now. "You, too."

"You look beautiful. Then again, you've always been a stunning woman. Bay is one lucky man."

The grin on her face faltered. Glancing away, she took a moment to compose herself, startled when Griff's hand gripped her chin, turning her toward him.

"Don't tell me that miscreant of a husband still hasn't come to his senses." He studied her face, letting his hand drop. "By the look on your face, he hasn't. Tell me about it, Suz."

She waited until the server brought them a bottle of wine, filled two glasses, and took their orders. "It shouldn't come as a surprise. He's refused to listen to anything I have to say about that night." Taking a sip of wine, she stared into the distance. "Until this afternoon."

Leaning toward her, he lifted a brow, waiting.

"We met so he could explain the divorce documents. Instead, he wanted me to tell him about that night." She cast a furtive gaze at one of the few people who knew the entire story, the horrid events which led to this point in her life. "You have no idea how he's treated me since I arrived in Conviction, Griff."

Suzette continued to sip her wine, explaining Bay's actions, seeing the look of surprise on their friend's face. She didn't tell him all of it. There was no reason to create a wedge between two men who'd been friends for so long. She'd always thought they were like bookends. Both from wealthy families, attended law school together, and instead of becoming attorneys, chose the profession of guns for hire. They were also about the same age, height, and build. Bay and Griffin could easily be mistaken for brothers.

"His request caught me off guard. After all the hurt, I never expected him to ask for my recollection of that night." She touched a finger to her temple, deciding not to divulge Bay's wish to put the past behind them. "I told him it was too late."

The server arrived, stalling Griff's reply. Setting plates of steak, potatoes, and beans in front of each of them, he stepped away. "Anything else, Miss Gasnier?"

She offered a wan smile. "This is fine. Thank you."

Griff's brow quirked. "Miss Gasnier?"

Sighing, she picked up her fork. "It's how I've been addressed since arriving in town. A few people know of our connection, but..." Her mouth twisted, remembering the night she'd told the latest of Bay's women they were married. "I did happen to introduce myself as Mrs. Donahue to the woman he brought in for supper the other night."

Griff stopped the fork midway to his mouth, set it down, and laughed. "Wish I'd have been there."

"He was a little distraught." She choked out a chuckle. "I shouldn't have done it. My outburst served no purpose and actually plays into what Bay wants."

"Would reconciling be so bad, Suz?"

Biting her lower lip, she rolled the stem of her glass between her fingers. "I don't know how it could be achieved. The town believes we're both single. Bay's made no secret of the women he's brought to his house. Nothing we've done indicates we have a connection beyond the hotel and restaurant. After all this time, how are we to announce that we're married?" She shook her head.

Rubbing his stubbled chin, Griff watched her. "The Suz I know wouldn't care what others thought. The same as she didn't care that Bay was a gunslinger. You married him regardless of the way he made a living."

She stared down at her lap. "I loved him."

Griff refilled his glass, leaning back in his chair. "And I'm guessing you still love him."

Pushing aside the truth of his words, Suzette let out a shaky breath. "I'll always love Bay." As much as she sometimes hated him, she didn't try to deceive herself. He was, and would always be, the love of her life.

"Perhaps..." The rest stalled in Griff's throat, his eyes shifting to movement at the front. Slowly, he pushed from his char, his stance and features rigid, hands loose at his sides.

"I didn't know you were in town, Griff." Bay stopped a couple feet away, staring at his friend, then Suzette.

Bay's soft voice and cool demeanor didn't fool either Suzette or Griffin. They'd seen him this way in the past and knew to be careful. Griffin held out his hand, not taking his gaze from Bay.

"Just rode in and decided to eat before finding you. Why don't you join your wife and me?" Griff waited, feeling the tension rise, then dissipate when Bay grasped his hand.

"Are you sure my *wife* doesn't mind?" He sent a meaningful look at Suzette.

She refused to give him the satisfaction of seeing her discomfort. "It's fine with me. Have you eaten?" When he shook his head, she saw the weariness in his eyes, the tight pull to his mouth, and the way his thick, dark hair seemed more disheveled than normal. "Are you feeling all right, Bay?"

Instead of lowering himself with his usual grace, he almost fell into the chair, grasping the edge of the table. "I'm fine."

"You look—"

"I'm fine, Suzette. Let it be." A trembling hand speared through his hair, doing nothing to improve the tousled appearance or flash of pain in his eyes.

She cast a quick glance at Griff, seeing the same concern in his eyes. "May I order you the same as what we're having?"

Pulling his chair closer to the table, he nodded. "That's fine."

"Wine or whiskey?"

He held up his hand. "Nothing more for me, Suzette." Bay didn't look at her as he spoke, his attention moving to Griff. "What brought you all the way to Conviction?"

"Let's wait until you've eaten, then we'll talk."

Mouth twisting in impatience, Bay nodded.

Taking another sip of wine, Griff focused on his friend. "Still glad you hung up your guns for practicing law?"

"Mostly. There are days I miss the hunt, but not the inevitable end."

Griff gave a curt nod, his expression sobering. "I understand."

Bay waited as the server placed his meal in front of him and left. "Are you thinking of giving it up?"

"Considering it."

Bay cut into his steak, chewing a bite while doing his best to not let Suzette's presence get to him. When they'd met earlier, his tight control had been all that stopped him from reaching out and pulling her into his arms.

He'd been surprised she'd turned down his request to talk about Calvan and what happened. Bay thought she'd be relieved at having the chance to explain. Instead, she'd thrown his past actions back at him, refusing to talk or even consider holding off on the divorce. On impulse, he'd torn up the documents, not surprised at the tinge of red spreading up her face.

She could ask August to help her, but knew his partner and friend wouldn't place himself between them. Other than a couple other lawyers, who mainly took on disorderly conduct cases, she'd be forced to go to Sacramento or San Francisco to find someone to petition for divorce. A divorce Bay knew she'd have almost no chance of obtaining.

"Bay. Are you still with us?"

Griff's voice cut through his thoughts. "Sorry. It's been a long day. What would you do if you stopped hiring out?"

Shrugging, he poured a little more wine into Suzette's glass and his. "I'm not sure. Law makes the most sense. I'm just not sure being in an office most of the day is right for me." Sipping his drink, he chuckled. "Guess I could become a professional gambler."

Suzette laughed. "Don't be ridiculous. Even I can beat you at cards, Griff."

Placing a hand against his chest, he feigned a hurt expression. "I've gotten better since you left St. Louis."

Smiling, she reached over, placing a hand on Griff's arm, a gesture Bay didn't miss. "If you intend to make a living by gambling, I hope you've gotten a *whole* lot better."

Finishing his meal, Bay sat back, envious at the easy banter between Suzette and Griff. He missed so much about their early marriage. Waking up with her, going to sleep with Suzette in his arms. Making love to his wife, the woman he wanted now with the same intensity as when they'd married.

"Now that we're done, tell me why you're here, Griff."

Smile slipping, his friend glanced at Suzette, then back at Bay. "It might be best to talk at your place."

Sliding her chair back, she stood, motioning to the men to stay seated. "Go ahead and talk. I need to check on the kitchen and make certain we're ready to lock up for the night. I hope to see you again before you leave town, Griff."

Standing, he leaned over, kissing her cheek. "You can depend on seeing me again, Suz."

Without sparing Bay a glance, she turned toward the kitchen, the sway of her hips driving him crazy. He turned a hard glare at Griff. "She is still my wife."

Relaxing in his chair, he lifted one shoulder. "For how long, Bay? If you want her back, seems to me you'd be working harder to get her back in your bed."

"What does that mean?"

"From what I've heard, you've done all you can to make both your lives miserable." He rolled the wine glass between his fingers, ignoring Bay's menacing stare. "Assuming you still love her, it may be time to listen to her side."

Bay shook his head, expelling a tired breath. "I tried today. She refused."

"You giving up after one attempt? If you are, I'll be the first in line to go after her."

Jaw clenching, Bay's nostrils flared, the anger subsiding when he saw the amusement in Griff's eyes. "Then I'd have to kill you."

Chuckling, Griff finished his wine before his face sobered. "Calvan's hired a man to get to you."

The news had Bay stiffening. "Where'd you hear this?"

"From Dave Calvan himself. The man can't help talking when he drinks, and he drank a lot a few weeks ago in Santa Fe."

Bay's brows drew together. "Santa Fe?"

"I heard a couple of his men say they were heading west to find you. It didn't take more than a minute for me to decide to follow. For some reason, he's never connected you and me, and since I'd planned to hunt you down myself, it made sense to follow him at the same time." Griff rested his arms on the table, leaning forward. "Look, Bay. I know what you *think* you saw, and I know what the doctor and sheriff learned. I also know Suz. You need to hear it from her, but any fool could see it was a setup to get back at you for killing Calvan's brother."

Scrubbing a hand down his face, he looked back at Griff, guilt consuming him. "Fine. He got back at me through Suzette. Why would he ride all this way for more?"

"First, he wanted to humiliate you. Drive you and Suz apart. It worked just like the ornery cuss planned. Appears that wasn't enough, though. Now he wants you dead, and if he gets your widow in the process..." Griff shrugged, letting his meaning settle in. "From what I heard, he's already got a man in Conviction. I don't know why or what the man plans to do, just that Calvan hired him. That alone makes it a bad deal for you, my friend."

Bay had to agree. "Who is this man?"

"I have no idea. What I do know is Calvan wants to be the one to kill you, so whatever the man is doing, he doesn't plan to put you in your grave."

"Doesn't make me feel any better." His thoughts turned to Suzette. "What about my wife?"

Griff's jaw tightened. "I don't know."

Murmuring an oath, Bay stood, grabbing the back of the chair to steady himself.

Griff jumped up, putting a hand on Bay's back. "Hey, you all right?"

Rubbing a hand over his forehead, he gave a terse nod. "Yeah. A little dizzy is all. I had a few drinks in the office before coming over here." He waved a hand through the air. "It's nothing."

"You seem a little unsteady."

"It'll pass. It always does."

Griff cocked his head. "What do you mean it *always* does? Has this happened before?"

Again, Bay waved him off. "A couple times. Where are you staying?"

A tentative grin turned up the corners of Griff's mouth. "I'm hoping to stay at your place."

"Good. You ready to head there or do you want to stop at the saloon?"

"Your place, Bay. Then you can tell me why you've been such a sonofabitch to Suz."

Chapter Seven

Brodie sat atop his horse, Colt and Sam on either side of him as they scanned the small house a hundred yards away. They'd ridden out of town at dawn, hoping the location they had for Maria Smith was accurate.

It had taken longer than Brodie expected to track down the woman believed to be the sister of Andrés Delgado. Their plan had been to locate her, then keep watch until her brother arrived with the money the woman needed for her family. If what they'd learned proved accurate, Andrés visited at least once each month, and Brodie meant to keep men posted until he arrived.

Their search for Ev Hunt, the Outlaw Doc, had proved less successful. He'd last been seen in Martinez, a town west of Conviction. A few days later, a man known to have won big at the gambling tables had been beaten, all his money gone. He might not have made it back to town if Hunt hadn't left his horse a quarter of a mile away. An odd occurrence for an outlaw, but consistent with what Colt had told them about the bandit.

"There." Sam pointed to the front, watching the door open and a woman walk outside. "Does she fit the description, Colt?"

Retrieving field glasses from his saddlebag, Colt peered through them, watching as the woman started her chores. "She matches what I know." He handed them to Brodie. "Do you recognize her?"

After a moment, Brodie lowered the glasses. "Nae. The lass looks small from here. Almost frail." He passed the field glasses to Sam.

"She's short and thin as a reed." He handed them back to Colt. "We can't be certain until Delgado shows. If he doesn't, we'll know it's been a waste of time. What do your instincts tell you, Brodie?" Sam had learned to listen to his brother-in-law's gut feelings.

"Aye. She's the one we're after."

Colt studied the woman one more time before sliding the field glasses back into the saddlebag. "She might recognize one of you, but not me. I'll ride up and confirm who she is. If she is Delgado's sister, we'll figure how to keep watch on her."

Kicking his horse, Colt emerged from the cover of the trees, riding straight toward the small, wooden structure. Releasing his badge, he slid it into a pocket. His gaze roamed the area around the homestead, not wanting to be caught unaware if Delgado hid in the distance.

The woman must have heard him approach because she whipped around from feeding the chickens to stalk toward him, waving her hand to warn him off. Instead, he continued forward.

"You are not welcome here. Go!" Her Spanish heritage came through in her voice.

"All I'm looking for is a drink of water—"

Shaking her head, she took a tentative step closer. "You must go." Her gaze jerked behind and around him in panic, her back rigid.

Colt looked around. Seeing no one, he dismounted. "A little water and I'll be gone."

Glaring at him, she blurted out a few words of Spanish, then stomped to a barrel by the front door. Turning, she motioned for him to follow. When he joined her on the small porch, she handed him a ladle full of water, which he swallowed in a few gulps.

"Thank you, Mrs..."

Taking the ladle from his outstretched hand, she set it aside. "Señora Smith," she muttered, followed by more words of Spanish.

Colt stifled a grin of satisfaction. "Thank you, Señora Smith. I'm grateful for the water." Without waiting for a response, he returned to his horse and swung into the saddle. Reining away, he looked over his shoulder, touching a finger to the brim of his hat.

He rode out in the opposite direction where Brodie and Sam waited, glancing around the surrounding area one more time. Making a wide arc, he took his time returning to where the other two lawmen stood next to their horses.

"It's Maria Smith, and she wasn't too friendly."

Sam nodded. "I wouldn't be either if my brother was an outlaw who might show up at any time. At least we know who she is."

Colt looked behind them, no longer seeing her from his spot between the trees. "Not only wasn't she welcoming, she kept looking around as if expecting someone. She seemed afraid."

Brodie swung into his saddle. "Aye. The lass doesn't want Delgado to discover her with a stranger. It may mean she expects the lad soon."

"I'll take the first watch. Three days?" Colt sent a questioning look at Brodie.

"Nae. Two days is enough before I send Alex or Seth. They're anxious to do something besides sit outside the jail or make turns around town."

"What about Jack?" Sam asked, mentioning Jack Perkins, the deputy who'd been with Brodie the longest.

Brodie chuckled. "The lad is enthusiastic, but I'm afraid he'd not be able to stay hidden and quiet for forty-eight hours. Nae, he'd give us away before sunset the first day."

Sam grinned, knowing Brodie was right. "I'll come out. That'll be four of us to split the watch."

Again, Brodie shook his head. "Nae, Sam. Jinny would have my head if you were gone for two days. Especially now with her carrying a wee bairn." His sister took care of her stepson, Robbie, and also kept watch on Sam's elderly father, Thomas.

Grimacing, Sam nodded. "She'd shoot us both for sure."

"There's no need for either of you to take turns. You have families who need you. Alex, Seth, and I can do this without your help." Colt slid to the ground.

"I'll have Seth or Alex ride out with enough food for the next couple days."

Colt gave Brodie a crisp nod. "Thanks."

He watched Sam and Brodie ride away as he pulled out each of his six-shooters, making sure the cylinders were loaded. Shoving them back into their holsters, he took out his field glasses to take another look around.

As before, nothing set off any of the warnings he often felt when allowing his instincts to take over. Instead, the day stretched before him as peaceful as when they'd ridden in over an hour ago. All he had to do now was wait for Delgado to appear. When the outlaw did, Colt would arrest him, then begin a more intensive search for Ev Hunt, the Outlaw Doc.

Ev watched the comings and goings on Conviction's main street, enjoying his breakfast of fried eggs, potato cakes, buttermilk biscuits, and wild berry shrub. He hadn't eaten such a good meal since leaving Martinez. It might be he'd find better food at the restaurant partially owned by Bay Donahue, but he'd purposely avoided the more posh establishment.

It wouldn't do for the retired gunslinger to recognize him, even though Ev believed the possibility slim. If what Calvan said could be trusted, Donahue had no idea of the Outlaw Doc's existence or his reason for being in Conviction.

The tall, slender outlaw had shaved off his light brown beard and trimmed his auburn hair, characteristics prominent on the wanted posters scattered around the west. Instead of the dark pants, coat, and vest he preferred, Ev wore the garb of a successful rancher. Even he didn't recognize himself.

He'd been so lost in watching what went on outside, Ev didn't hear the boots on the wood floor until they stopped by his table. Looking up, he first noticed the badge, then moved his gaze to the man's face.

"I don't believe we've met. I'm Seth Montero, one of the deputies." He held out his hand.

Standing, Ev grasped it, studying the man before him. "Bill Jones. It's a pleasure."

Seth's gaze narrowed as he studied the man's face. Something about him seemed familiar. "Are you looking for work or passing through?"

Ev's mouth drew into a thin line. "I'm a rancher near Sacramento. I've got some business up this way." He hoped the vague answer would be enough to send the deputy on his way.

Seth didn't have any reason to continue questioning him. Still, his gut twisted in a way he couldn't explain. "Hope you enjoy your stay in Conviction, Mr. Jones."

Turning away, he continued to a table, taking a seat facing Jones. Seth's gaze lingered on him, trying to figure out why he seemed familiar, what caused the pulse of recognition. Several minutes later, Jones paid and left, not sparing Seth another glance.

He continued studying Jones as he crossed the street and passed between two buildings. Once out of sight, Seth quickly finished his breakfast before leaving for the jail. He needed to go through the wanted posters. Somewhere in the stack of papers Seth believed he'd find the answer to the questions he had about Jones.

Bay struggled to stay focused on the work in front of him, rubbing his temples every few minutes to relieve the pressure. He'd woken with the same pounding in his head and churning in his stomach which had plagued him for days.

It would've seemed normal except he'd downed only two glasses of whiskey in his office the day before. He hadn't swallowed another drop during supper with Griff, and nothing else after they'd gone home. At least he hadn't experienced more tingling in his hands that morning, although when he'd first gotten out of bed, his feet felt numb for several minutes.

Drawing a hand down his face, Bay tried again to concentrate on a contract for the purchase of land between Conviction and Settlers Valley. It wasn't complicated. Still, he couldn't focus on the document for more than a minute at a time.

A soft knock drew his attention. Grateful for the interruption, he stood and walked to the door as another knock sounded. Drawing the door open, his body stilled at the sight of the woman waiting in the hall.

He allowed his gaze to move over Suzette, taking in her beauty, the way her features softened when she saw him. A softness he hadn't seen in much too long. Instead of welcoming her, his mouth curled into a rueful scowl.

"I don't recall having an appointment with you this morning."

Suzette's open features closed at his terse comment. Lifting her chin, she glared at him.

"We don't." Instead of waiting for him to stand aside, she stepped forward, brushing past him. "Regardless, it's time we talked. Afterward, you can prepare the divorce documents. I'll sign and we'll be done with it."

Bay's heart sank at her words. After hours of talking with Griff the night before, he'd realized how much of a fool he'd been. Griff had given him enough information, what his friend had learned from the doctor and sheriff, for Bay to understand Calvan's intent. What Griff didn't know was Suzette's version. He hadn't been in St. Louis when it all happened, and by the time Griff returned, Bay had fled and Suzette had slipped into a world she let no one enter.

Closing the door, he stepped forward, stopping a few inches away. "No."

Her eyes flashed. "What do you mean *no*?"

Crossing his arms, Bay's determined gaze didn't waver. "I'm no longer interested in ending our marriage." His hand lifted to cup the back of her neck. Before she understood his intention, his head lowered, warm lips brushing across hers, voice softening. "I still want you, Suzette." He whispered the words against her lips before placing another kiss on her mouth. Stepping away, he watched confusion, anger, and perhaps a slight amount of hope cross her face.

Touching a finger to her lips, Suzette closed her eyes a moment before opening them to search Bay's face. "After all that's happened, the way you've treated me, why are you doing this now?" Her voice cracked on the last before she glanced away, fighting to control her emotions.

His gut clenched at the stark regret in her voice. Regret he'd caused by his stubborn insistence to push her aside, not willing to hear her side of the story. Guilt pierced through him, remembering what Griff had told him, wondering what else he'd learn from Suzette.

Pulling out a chair at the small table, he waited until she sat down, taking a seat next to her. Exhaling a slow breath, he leaned forward, wanting to take her hand in his but resisting.

"It took me this long to realize what a fool I've been. I don't want a divorce, Suzette."

She bit her bottom lip so it wouldn't tremble. "What do you want?"

Bay didn't hesitate. "You."

Brows furrowed, Suzette shook her head, unable to grasp his meaning. "But all you've done is shun and demean me since that night. There must be more, Bay. I see no reason you should want me back in your life now."

"It's quite simple. I want a family, children with someone who is compatible with me. I've no reason to search for another woman when I already have a wife who fills my every need. You're also beautiful and smart. And we know we're well-suited in bed." He controlled the grimace he felt as the words tumbled forth. Everything he'd said was true. Once spoken, they sounded cold and calculating, not the words of a man who cared at all about his wife.

The longer he spoke, the larger the ball of ice in her stomach felt. He'd not talked of love or wanting her back because he'd wrongly convicted her in his mind. Anger rising, she clenched her jaw, not wanting to spew her disgust at his sorry reasons for reconciliation.

"Let me understand this. You don't want the divorce because it would force you to start over in a search for someone to fulfill your long list of qualifications."

"Suzette..."

Standing, she stared down at him, fury flaring in her dark emerald green eyes. She settled fisted hands on her hips, still not quite believing what she'd heard him say. "I mistakenly thought you wanted me back because you still love me and want to hear the truth of what happened with Calvan." She blew away an errant strand of hair, which had fallen across her face.

"Suzette..."

"Don't say any more, Bay. I'm not a stupid twit who's willing to settle for so little after the true marriage we had before." She sucked in a breath, willing herself to calm down. "Before you shoved me out of your life. Well, you'll have to take the time to find another woman because this one wants no part in the callous future you seek. People may scorn me because of our divorce, but at least I'll take satisfaction in knowing I did what was right, even if you see my actions as a personal betrayal." Turning her back to him, she stomped to the door. "Rewrite the documents and give them to August. I'll be back tomorrow morning to sign them."

Jumping to his feet, Bay grabbed her wrist as she reached her hand toward the doorknob. "Don't go. Please. Let me try to explain."

Chest heaving in frustration, she shook her head. "You were already quite eloquent." Swallowing, she lifted her haunted gaze to meet his. "Please, Bay. Let me go. You'll never forgive me, never love me the way you once did. I just want..." She put a hand to her stomach, not wanting him to see the depth of her pain.

He kept his grip on her wrist, his voice soft and soothing. "You just want what?"

"I just want the ache in my heart to stop."

Chapter Eight

Instead of letting go, Bay drew Suzette into his arms, feeling her tremble as quiet sobs escaped. He felt helpless. The wife he remembered never cried, showed no weakness of any kind. She'd been tough and determined, yet always a lady. Nothing stopped Suzette from reaching for her goal of becoming a chef and managing a restaurant.

She'd come to Conviction to pursue her dream, even if it meant Bay reentering her life. No matter what he did, how he hurt or humiliated her, she'd worn a smile, done her work with true proficiency.

For the first time, Bay understood what his selfish actions had done to her. His face burned with shame, gut twisting when she sobbed again. Suzette had slipped her arms around his waist, resting her head against his chest. He couldn't describe how good it felt to have his wife back in his arms.

Rubbing Suzette's back, he rested his chin on her head. "I'm sorry, sweetheart. So very sorry."

When her arms tightened around him, Bay pressed a kiss to her temple. To his surprise, she didn't pull away, providing a slight amount of hope. He brushed another kiss across her cheek and waited. Emboldened, but not wanting to take advantage, he pulled back.

Looking down at her tear-streaked face and puffy eyes, he cupped her face with both hands. One heartbeat passed, then another before Bay lowered his head, gently claiming her mouth. At the feel of her hands gripping his wrists, he intensified the pressure on her soft, full lips, feeling his body respond. He hated to end the contact, but understood their future could depend on what he did right now. Raising his mouth, Bay stared down into languid eyes.

Lowering his hands to her shoulders, he made a quick decision. "I need to talk to August for a minute. Don't leave." He dropped his arms, his gaze intensifying. "Please don't leave, Suzette."

Confusion clouded her features before she looked away, giving no commitment.

Bay gripped her chin, turning her back to face him. "Suzette?" His pleading gaze locked with hers. He watched as she swallowed, a flash of concern crossing her face.

"All right. But only for a few minutes."

Dipping his head, he gave her a quick kiss. "One minute is all I need." He left his office, crossing the short distance to August's. As he'd agreed, he rejoined Suzette sixty seconds later.

He found her at the window, staring at the street below with her arms banded around her waist. Clearing his throat so as not to startle her, he stepped next to her, threading his fingers through hers.

"Spend the rest of the day with me, Suzette. We'll ride out of town. There's something I want to show you."

Holding his breath, he followed her gaze out the window toward the livery.

"I have to be at work in an hour."

"Not today."

She shifted to look at him. "What do you mean?"

"I spoke with August. He's glad to see you take an evening off. He'll take care of everything at the restaurant."

Rounding on him, her eyes sparked. "You can't do that. I *need* the work, Bay." She turned to walk away when a strong hand gripped her arm.

"We need to talk and—"

"No, we don't need to talk. It's too late for that. I—" Her next words were cut off when Bay placed his fingers against her lips.

"No, it isn't too late. Not for us, Suzette."

Shoving his fingers away, she gave a slow shake of her head. "You've made no secret of how much you hate me."

"I don't hate you. I've never hated you." Stepping away, he ran a hand through his overlong hair, staring out the window for a moment before he returned his attention to her. Lips pinched, the lines around his eyes and mouth appeared deeper than she remembered. "Come with me, Suzette. Please."

He held out his hand, waiting, hoping she'd stop fighting him for a few hours. Bay saw the instant her features softened, the anger dissolving. A moment later, she reached out, threading her fingers through his.

Relief flooded him. It was a start, but Bay knew the worst was still before them. He also knew he wouldn't run this time. No matter what she had to say, how difficult it might be to hear, he'd listen.

Ev Hunt leaned a shoulder against the corner of a building, his mood improving the instant Bay walked outside, a beautiful woman on his arm. It took him a moment to realize the woman was Suzette Gasnier, the manager at the Feather River Hotel and its connecting restaurant.

The woman and where she worked meant nothing to Ev. At least not in connection with the job he'd accepted from Dave Calvan.

He'd first thought the man's request ridiculous. Weaken Bay to a point he'd be an easy target for Calvan. After a few weeks, Ev had seen the elegance of it. He'd also enjoyed witnessing Bay's deterioration. To most, it wouldn't be noticeable. To a doctor such as Hunt, it was a simple diagnosis. Regardless, for the money Calvan offered, the job was more enjoyable than any he'd taken in years.

Following them to the livery, he recognized the opportunity their leaving town presented. Ev didn't care where they went as long as they stayed away for at least an hour. He could get everything completed in a short period of time.

The moment they'd disappeared inside the livery, Ev turned around, a slight grin lifting the corners of his mouth.

Colt picked up the field glasses again, taking a slow sweep over the Smith homestead. So far, there'd been little action this morning, the same as yesterday. In his gut, he knew Delgado would appear. He just didn't know when or if he'd be alone.

The outlaw had a history of riding alone, or with one or two others. They were men he trusted and knew for years. Men who didn't run at the first sign of trouble. At least that was what his boss had told Colt. It didn't amount to much. Only a little better than nothing.

Setting the glasses down, he leaned his back against the tree trunk. From what he'd seen so far, there was no Mr. Smith. It made sense. If there had been a husband around, she probably wouldn't need the money her brother brought each month.

Pulling one knee up, he rested a wrist over it, continuing to watch the house. He hadn't slept well the night before, not wanting to miss a chance to catch Delgado if he did show. Colt believed he could take on a lone outlaw, but maybe not two or three. It would depend on if he caught them by surprise and if their skills with a gun weren't as good as his. He thought the chance of that slim.

Closing his eyes, Colt leaned his head against the tree. The soft breeze, leaves rustling in the wind, soothed him. Within minutes, he fell asleep.

The feel of someone kicking his boot and sound of quiet laughter woke him. Reflex had him lifting the gun from its holster, pointing it at the form standing in front of him.

"Damn, Alex. I could've shot you." Shaking his head, Colt pushed himself up, holstering the six-shooter.

The deputy gave an incredulous shake of his head. "Doubtful. If I'd been Delgado, you'd be dead."

Alex was right, and Colt knew it.

Walking a few feet toward the ranch house, the deputy scanned the area. "Has it been this quiet since Brodie and Sam left you here?"

Colt stepped beside him. "Yep. She and a couple children are all I've seen. They go in and out of the house throughout the day. No sign of Delgado, though."

"It could take weeks if he visited right before you found her. I think she's still the best chance we have of finding him."

Colt nodded. "I agree. You're here sooner than I expected."

"Brodie asked me to come early. He wants to meet with you about something. Didn't say what. Just asked that I send you back."

Brows furrowing, Colt gathered the little amount of gear, cinched his horse's saddle tighter, and mounted. "Don't try to be a hero, Alex. If Delgado rides in with other men, head back to town and get me."

Alex rubbed the stubble on his chin, his mouth twisting. "Didn't you say he doesn't stay long at his sister's? It might be our only chance to get him."

"Not if his other men shoot you." Reining his horse in a circle, he drew up. "I'm serious about this. If he approaches alone, the decision is yours. If not, ride for town." He waited until Alex nodded, then rode off, hoping the deputy heeded his advice.

"Where are we going?" Suzette rode next to Bay, enjoying riding again after so long not owning a horse. She'd rented one from the livery a few times, but it wasn't the same as having a horse of her own.

He smiled over at her, continuing north along the Feather River. "It's a surprise."

"How much farther is it?"

"Not long at all. Just around the bend in the river." Ever since they left town almost half an hour earlier, he'd kept sending cautious glances at her. Bay wouldn't have been surprised if she changed her mind and tried to get away from him. So far, the ride had been pleasant, as if nothing had ever happened between them.

Five minutes later, he reined to a stop. "Here we are."

Suzette looked around, not understanding what she was supposed to see. "What exactly am I looking at?"

"Our land. We own two thousand acres bounded by the MacLaren ranch and the Feather River." He swept his hand around as he spoke, the excitement in his voice evident. "We'll build a house, run some cattle, raise horses, whatever we want." Bay glanced at Suzette. "Whatever *you* want."

Her jaw dropped as she followed his gaze, not understanding. "What do you mean *our* land?"

Resting his hands on the saddlehorn, he continued to survey the property. "I drew up a contract so we own the land jointly. Not fifty-fifty, but together, Suzette."

She turned a baffled gaze toward him. "Why would you do that?"

Riding a few yards away from the river, he dismounted, then helped her down, letting his hands rest on her waist. "Because I want to do whatever I can to help us get back together." Leaning down, he brushed a kiss across her lips, then stepped away. "I know there's a good deal of hurt and anger between us, but I'm willing to try again if you are." Seeing tears well in her eyes, he pulled her into his arms. "Tell me you'll at least consider it."

Wrapping her arms around his waist, she rested her head on his chest. She thought of what Griff had said about her not caring what others thought as long as she had Bay. Until today, she'd thought their marriage over, ruined beyond repair.

"I don't understand what has changed in the last week. It wasn't long ago you brought another of your women into the restaurant. Why would you do that if you wanted to try again?"

Leaning away, he placed a finger under her chin, lifting her face to look into her eyes. "Because of some things you've said in the last few days." He let out a breath. "And because of what Griff told me about that night."

Her gaze narrowed in confusion. "What Griff told you?"

He pressed his mouth against hers, needing the contact, wanting much more. Drawing away, he took her hand, leading her several yards away. "He told me what he'd learned from the doctor and the sheriff. But I need to hear it all from you, as I should've done when I woke up from my injuries."

"Before you left me."

Letting out a haggard breath, he nodded. "Before I made what I believe to be the worst mistake of my life."

Her gaze searched his, hope and love flaring in her eyes. "And if you don't like what I tell you?"

"All I'm looking for is the truth, Suzette. I already know I won't like what you'll have to say, but it won't matter. It won't be easy to hear, but at least I'll have the truth."

Stepping away, she paced toward a stand of trees surrounded by large rocks and low brush. In the clearing close by, she saw a large meadow, wildflowers peeking up through thick, green grass. Lowering her head, she rubbed her temples, doing her best to understand what Bay had said.

Suzette definitely understood what he hadn't said. Love had not once crossed his lips. Even though she'd bared herself to him, admitted she still loved Bay, had always loved him, he hadn't reciprocated. Whipping around, she marched back to him, lifting her chin in a defiant gesture.

"Do you still love me, Bay?"

The tightness in his chest eased. "I've always loved you, Suzette."

Chapter Nine

"I was preparing supper, thinking about the trip we'd planned to Philadelphia." Suzette paced back and forth in front of where Bay leaned against a large boulder. "I'd received the telegram from you, saying to expect you that night." She glanced up at him. "I wanted to have something special ready when you got home."

Swallowing the bile in his throat, he nodded for her to continue.

"There was a loud pounding on the front door. When I opened it, Dave Calvan shoved me aside and entered, followed by three men. I tried to scream, but he stuffed a handkerchief into my mouth, bound my wrists, and hauled me upstairs." Her haunted gaze met his. "I tried to kick, but it was useless. The men only laughed at me. Looking back, it was stupid to open the door without grabbing a gun first." She shook her head. "There's so much I would change if I could."

When he pushed from the rock, meaning to walk up to her, she held up her hands, stopping his progress. "Let me get it all out, Bay. Please."

Jaw clenching, he nodded. "All right." He returned to his spot against the boulder.

Resuming her pacing, Suzette clenched her hands at her sides. "Somehow, they knew you'd be back that night. Calvan said if I didn't do what I was told, they'd kill us both. It was my decision if you lived or died." Sucking in a ragged breath, she continued. "Calvan ordered one man to hide in the wardrobe, another behind the door in the bedroom, and the third behind the curtains. While they hid, he ripped my dress, pulling it down so all I wore was my chemise." For a brief moment, she glanced over at him, her face lined in misery and what he believed to be regret. "He explained what he planned, then we waited. When we heard you enter the kitchen, he cut the rope around my wrists and pulled the handkerchief from my mouth. Then he drew a knife and pointed it at my stomach."

Striding several feet away, she stared at the ground, drawing in large gulps of air. After a few minutes, she turned back toward him.

"I'll never forget the look on your face when you stepped into our room. I remember closing my eyes and turning away. I didn't want you to see the pain and terror on my face." Suzette held her arms out, palms toward him. "If you saw my face, you'd know it was all a lie and Calvan's men would've killed you. I couldn't let that happen, Bay."

Wrapping her arms around her waist, she worked to control the agony of reliving the worst night of her life. "When you moved toward the bed, one of his men came up behind you, slamming the butt of his gun on your head. The other two emerged from their hiding places, kicking and punching you. Calvan shoved me aside, joining his men. I remember screaming, rushing toward them, but my efforts were wasted. Calvan backhanded me, slamming me against a wall. I remember pain shooting through my head, then nothing."

Trying to approach Suzette again, he stopped when she shook her head. "Someone heard my screams and ran for the sheriff. I don't remember anything else until I woke in the clinic. I was in one bed and you were beside me, looking so broken and bloody. I thought you were dead, Bay. No matter what Doc did, he couldn't pull you from unconsciousness. He tried to tell me it was for the best, that if you did wake, you'd never be the man you once were. You'd have brain damage and might not regain the use of your hands."

A mirthless chuckle crossed her lips. "I told him he was wrong and I'd never give up on you. I stayed by your bed for days, talking to you, trying to get broth down your throat, holding your hand. Then one morning several days later, I woke up and you were gone." Her agonized gaze met his, slicing him as if she wielded a sword.

"No one knew where you went or how you got out of the clinic. I rushed home, ran from room to room calling your name. Then I saw the note on the kitchen table." She put a hand to her chest, trying to stop the too familiar pain at what she'd read. "I never imagined you'd turn on me, believe I'd be capable of betraying you. Not once did I consider you'd leave me."

Voice breaking, her lithe form trembled until she sank to the ground, sobbing in uncontrollable gasps. Covering her face with her hands, unable to stop the violent shaking of her body, Suzette felt herself being lifted, held against Bay's hard chest.

Bay walked to a fallen tree, lowering himself down, cradling her in his lap. "I'm so sorry, sweetheart. So very sorry." Rocking her back and forth, tears streamed down his face, his heart breaking at all the misery he'd caused by his callous actions.

Burying his face in her hair, Bay cursed himself over and over until he'd run out of vile words to describe what he'd done. He didn't deserve the woman in his arms, but he was a selfish sonofabitch who had no intention of ever letting her go again.

A wave of panic squeezed his chest at the thought she might not feel the same.

Running his hand down her silken hair, Bay inhaled a deep breath. He'd never been a man to pray when life became tough. Now, with Suzette in his arms, he couldn't stop talking to God, praying she'd forgive him, promising to make it up to her.

If she'd give him the chance.

As her sobs slowed, he felt her hand clasp the front of his shirt, her fingers digging through the fabric and into his skin. After a moment, she pulled back, looking up at him.

"I don't know what came over me." She sniffed, brushing moisture from her face. "I'm not normally one to cry."

A pained grin tilted the corners of his mouth. "It's all right, sweetheart." Leaning down, he pressed a soft kiss against her lips. "If I'd been a better man..." His voice trailed off. He closed his eyes, shaking his head in disgust. "Everything, all of what's happened the last two years, is my fault." Bay didn't understand the chuckle which escaped her lips. Looking down, his brows furrowed at the mischievous glint in her eyes.

"Well, yours and Calvan's." She wrapped her arms around his neck, fingers rifling through his thick tresses.

The humor in her voice gave him hope. "I can't argue with you."

Keeping her arms around his neck, she once again rested her head against his chest. "What do we do now, Bay?"

He'd been dreading the question, the one he knew needed to be answered. "Well, I believe that's what we need to figure out." Rubbing his hand idly over her back in a soothing, circular motion, he cleared his throat. "I love you, Suzette, but I've done and said things you might not ever be able to forgive."

"So you believe me?"

Murmuring a curse, he lifted her chin, his eyes full of remorse. "Yes. I'm so sorry I didn't stay in St. Louis to hear your story. Everything I put you through wouldn't have happened if I'd remained at the clinic instead of running." Again, he stroked her hair, pressing a kiss to the tip of her nose. "I'll understand if you still want the divorce, but you need to know I don't. I never have."

Brows knitting together, she straightened in his lap, one arm still wrapped around his neck while the other hand rested against his chest. "But you've made no secret about how much you can't stand the sight of me. And the women. You've been with so many, making certain I saw every one of them."

Touching her cheek with his thumb, he brushed away a fresh tear. The agony in her eyes cut through him like a knife.

"From the day we met until right now, I swear I've not been with another woman." Gritting his teeth, he tried to ignore the lump in his throat. It would take him a lifetime to make up for all the hurt he'd caused. "There's no excuse for all the mistakes I've made, the misery I've caused you. But you need to know not one of those women was ever invited into my bed. That place is still only for you, Suzette."

Lips parting, she blinked several times, eyes clouded in confusion. "But..."

"The same as you, I've never betrayed our wedding vows." His pleading gaze met hers. "I don't want a divorce, Suzette, but if you do, I'll understand. Whatever you want, even if it kills me, I'll do everything in my power to make certain you get it."

An uncontrollable shudder shot through her as a voice in her head warned her to be careful.

Seeing the confusion on her face, Bay sent up another prayer, hoping God heard. "I know the extent of the mess I've made. There is a solution, though."

Lifting a brow, she cocked her head to the side. "A solution?"

"To the biggest problem standing between us."

She gave a slow nod. "The fact most people don't know we're married and you've made no secret of all the women you've escorted around Conviction."

Bay almost choked on her wording. *All the women.* She was right. He'd been a pompous ass...and a fool. To save his marriage, he had to get her agreement to his plan.

"So, what is your solution, Bay?"

Sliding her off his lap and setting her next to him on the fallen log, he took her hands in his. He hadn't thought this through, but as soon as the idea slid across his mind, Bay knew it was right.

"Miss Suzette Gasnier, will you do me the great honor of allowing me to court you?"

At first, she didn't understand his intention, why he'd ask to court her when they were already married. Then her eyes widened, a knowing smile drawing up the corners of her mouth.

Lifting a brow, Bay squeezed her hands, working to keep the grin from his face. "What is your answer, Miss Gasnier?"

Biting her lower lip, she gave him an unhurried nod. "Mr. Donahue, I'd be flattered to have you court me."

Leaning forward, his lips touched hers for an instant before a hand slipped behind her neck to tug Suzette closer. Deepening the kiss, tasting her the way he'd wanted for much too long, he groaned in pleasure, hearing her moan in response.

Loosening his hold, he rested his forehead against hers, letting out a ragged breath.

"The last thing I want is to stop, sweetheart." Bay saw confusion flash across her face. "But this needs to be done right. You deserve time to make certain you can forgive all the horrid things I've done and said."

"Bay—"

He touched a finger to her lips while shaking his head. "I refuse to rush you, Suzette. We'll court until you're certain you can trust me again." He searched her face, hoping the chance he was taking would turn out as he hoped.

"And if I decide I *can* trust you?"

"Then, Miss Gasnier, you and I will get married. Again."

"I'm sorry, Mr. Jones, but Mr. Donahue isn't here." Jasper glanced down at a journal on his desk, shaking his head. "I don't believe he'll be back today. I'd be happy to schedule a meeting when it's convenient for you."

Ev tugged the cowboy hat lower on his forehead, hiding his features as much as possible. He'd used the same name as he'd given Jasper and the deputy in the restaurant. The same one he'd provided when registering at the Gold Dust Hotel down the street. Crossing his arms, he flashed Jasper an annoyed expression.

"If that's the best you can do. It will have to be next week, though."

"Of course." Flipping the pages of the journal, Jasper glanced up. "Next Wednesday at eleven. Will that suit?"

"Fine."

"Wonderful, Mr. Jones." Jasper jotted down the meeting, closing the journal.

Turning for the door, Ev reached into his pocket, walking back to the desk. "I've another bottle of whiskey for Mr. Donahue. I trust he enjoyed the other two."

Taking the bottle from his outstretched hand, Jasper nodded. "Oh, very much, Mr. Jones. I'll make certain Mr. Donahue gets this one as well."

Waving a hand in the air, he walked out into the darkening sky. He'd already accomplished the other errand he needed to complete before Bay returned from his ride with his lovely companion. Now all he could do was wait, hoping the results of all his work would soon materialize.

The sun made its final descent behind the western hills as Bay and Suzette rode into the livery and dismounted. They'd talked almost another hour at his new property. *Their* property, as he'd pointed out more than once while they discussed ideas for building a house and a barn, populating the pastures with cattle and horses. Two thousand acres for them to do whatever they wanted.

Bay handed the reins of each horse to the blacksmith who came out to greet them. Placing a hand on the small of Suzette's back, he guided her down the street where both of their residences were located, only two houses separating them. They reached hers first, Suzette turning toward him.

"For the most part, I had a wonderful time, Bay." One corner of her mouth quirked upward when he lifted a brow. "Your property is—"

"*Our* property."

Every time he'd mentioned it being theirs, her heart seized, a rush of hope taking hold. Each time, Suzette ruthlessly shoved the optimism aside. She couldn't afford to count on him too much. Not anymore. It had been too easy for him to disregard her love when he found her with Calvan, waiting until now to hear her side.

"*Our* property is beautiful."

Stroking his hand down her arm, he moved a few inches closer. "And the rest?"

Licking her lips, Suzette pulled her gaze away from his, watching as several people passed, barely noticing them. "Are you asking about your idea to court?"

Moving closer, he forced her back until she bumped into the house's front door. "All of it, Suzette." Keeping his voice just above a whisper, he rested a hand against the door above her head, leaning down. "I understand this may not be easy for you. Trusting me again will take time."

She swallowed, her body heating at his closeness, making it hard to develop a clear thought. He'd always been able to read her emotions, the slight changes in expression, the way her body would tense or relax in different circumstances. Nothing had changed.

Shrugging, she let out a slow breath. "You're right. I am willing to try again, Bay."

"But you can't make any promises."

Looking at the ground, she shook her head. "Not yet. It will take time." Lifting her head, she met his gaze. "And what if, after a while, you realize I'm no longer who you want?"

"Suzette—"

"Please, Bay, let me finish." Her voice was low, beseeching. "It was easy for you to turn your back on me before."

Nostrils flaring, he shook his head. "It was *not* easy," he growled. "Why do you think I haven't bedded another woman since you?"

"I don't—"

Bay closed the distance between them. "Because you are the only woman I want. It's always been you, Suzette. It will *always* be you." Brushing his thumb over her lower lip, he let out a remorseful sigh. "We'll court because that's what you need to trust me again. If it was my decision, we'd be at the church right now."

Eyes widening a little, her lips parted as he continued to stroke his thumb over her soft, plump lip.

"I'll give you as much time as you need. Weeks, months, years. Whatever you need, Suzette. I'm never losing sight of the most important part of my life."

"Which is?"

Bay swept a quick kiss across her lips, unmindful of anyone watching. "You."

Chapter Ten

Closing the door of Suzette's house after she disappeared inside, Bay ignored the guilt at not returning to his office. Instead, he walked past Sam's house, then August's before reaching his own, running a tired hand through his hair as he entered.

It had taken Bay a good bit of coaxing to talk Suzette into letting him escort her to supper at the Great West Café. It would be their first time out in public as a couple trying to decide if they had a future. The smaller restaurant at the end of Conviction's main street would allow them to relax, eat an excellent meal, and talk. Although he didn't know what else they could say after the revelations of the day.

Bay understood Suzette's hesitancy at allowing him to get close to her again. If their roles had been reversed, he didn't know if he'd even consider it. She was a better person than him, had always provided light in a cold world, compassion when others would turn away. And she'd saved his life.

Now, he wanted her to save him in a different way. Their time apart had been the worst period of his life. When August hired Suzette to manage the hotel and restaurant, Bay had been furious, but believed his partner didn't know the relationship between them. He now understood August knew more about what happened that night than Bay.

His friend had intentionally brought her to Conviction not just to run their business, but with the hope she and Bay would reconcile. Thinking on it, he had to chuckle, grateful beyond measure for the meddling older man. He needed to thank him, but Bay would wait until he and Suzette had more time together.

Hanging his gunbelt on the hook, he walked to a cabinet, pulling down a bottle of whiskey. Pouring a large measure, Bay took a sip, then downed the rest in a few swallows. As the amber liquid burned a path down his throat, he studied the bottle, remembering Griff had finished a bottle last night and there'd been no more in the house. Shrugging, he set it back inside the cabinet. Griff rode to Settlers Valley that morning, but when he returned, Bay would thank him. Afterward, they'd have a serious discussion with August about Griff joining the law practice.

Taking the stairs two at a time, Bay stumbled on the last one, falling forward to land on his knees. Hissing out a string of curses, his head began to pound, stomach churning. Trying to stand, he rolled into a sitting position, resting his arms across bent knees, blinking at the multiple images that appeared before him.

"Damn." Rubbing his temples, Bay grabbed the banister, pulling himself up to stand. He'd never had a problem with the stairs before, not even when he'd spent the night drinking and playing cards at Buckie's Castle.

Having no time to sort it out before changing clothes and walking back to Suzette's, he put the mishap behind him.

Suzette stood at her front window, arms crossed, staring outside at the darkening street. Cleaning up and changing into clean clothes hadn't taken long, giving her time to think about the events of the day.

Her mind reeled with the change in Bay. His feelings reversed in such a short period, she found it hard to accept. Last week he hated her, or acted as if he did. Today he spoke of love and not wanting the divorce. It was almost more than Suzette could accept.

Worse, she couldn't quell the fear he'd return to the Bay of the last couple years, reviling her for the actions which saved him. After all, he'd done it once already, finding it all too easy to leave her behind at the first threat to their marriage. He'd let his emotions rule, not considering there might be more to the scene in their bedroom.

Drawing the drapes closed, she turned toward the parlor, the sense of loss still as strong as before meeting him in his office today. Suzette couldn't quite place why his turnaround bothered her so much. Perhaps she'd feel more at peace if she understood why he finally made the decision to hear her side, and consider changing his treatment of her.

She'd never expected him to announce plans to court her, with the ultimate goal of marrying. The thought would've made her chuckle if she wasn't so confused. Admittedly, it was an elegant solution to the problem which haunted her.

After all he'd so publicly forced her to endure, how would the announcement they'd been married for years be accepted? Suzette knew the answer. Most in town wouldn't accept it. The gossip would be swift, the good people of Conviction condemning them both.

Before she could lower herself into her favorite chair, a rap on the door had her turning. Unless Bay decided to come for her early, she didn't expect any callers. Opening the door, a smile broke across her face.

"Griff." Stepping aside, Suzette motioned him inside. "I wasn't expecting you."

Removing his hat, he stopped beside her, placing a kiss on her cheek. "I hope I'm not intruding."

"Not at all." Moving back to the parlor, she picked up a decanter. "Whiskey?"

"Please." Glancing around, his gaze landed on the most substantial piece of furniture in the room.

"You won't break anything." She chuckled at the way his big frame dwarfed the graceful furniture.

Quirking a brow, he accepted the glass she offered. "Are you certain?"

He waited until she sat down before starting to lower himself onto a slender wooden chair, the seat and back covered with tapestry upholstery.

A somber expression crossed her face. "Well, it hasn't happened to anyone yet."

Hesitating, he glanced up before his weight would've settled onto the seat. "Yet?"

Laughing, she motioned for him to sit down. "I'm joking. Do sit down and tell me what brought you by this evening."

"I heard Bay and you went riding." Griff swallowed some of the whiskey, a slight grin appearing. "This is quite good. Anyway, I wanted to make certain you were all right."

"All right?"

His lips thinned. "Did he say anything distressing, Suz?"

"Distressing? No. Confusing? Yes."

Leaning forward, he adjusted himself on the small chair. "Confusing in what way?"

Staring down at the clasped hands in her lap, she felt another wave of uncertainty wash through her. Standing, Suzette paced a few feet away before turning back. "He asked me to explain what happened with Calvan."

"That couldn't have been easy."

Drawing in a breath, she shook her head. "No, it wasn't. He did listen, though. Afterward, Bay said he didn't want the divorce." A tremor flickered in her jaw. "He wants to court me."

Griff choked on the last swallow of whiskey. "Court you? What for when you're already married?"

Stifling a bemused grin, Suzette explained their concern about the women he'd escorted around town, the damage it would do to suddenly announce they'd been married for quite a while.

"I do believe the most important reason is Bay wants me to be certain I'll be able to trust him again."

Nodding, he set the empty glass aside. "And can you?"

Lifting one shoulder in a shrug, her features held a touch of sadness. "I don't know."

Pushing out of the chair, Griff strolled to stand next to her. "Bay loves you, Suz."

"Maybe." The doubt in her voice broke his heart.

"There's no maybe to it." Placing a hand on her shoulder, Griff drew her into his arms. "The man's besotted with you, has been from the moment he spotted you in St. Louis." Pulling away, he took a step backward, leaving his hands resting on her shoulders. "Give him a chance to prove it to you."

"It's not about him loving me, Griff. It's about trust."

Dropping his hands to his sides, he offered an encouraging grin. "I'd trust him with my life, Suz."

A soft snort burst through her lips. "But you don't have to trust him with your heart." Both turned at knocking on her door. "That will be Bay. He's taking me to supper."

Griff headed toward the door. "Starting the courting tonight, is he?" Opening the door, he squelched a grin at the shock on Bay's face.

"What the hell are you doing here?" Pushing past him, Bay walked straight to Suzette, hitching a thumb toward Griff. "When did he get here?"

Crossing her arms, she shot him a look of displeasure. "A few minutes ago, not that it's any of your business."

Jaw clenching, Bay turned toward Griff. "So, why are you here with my..."

Chuckling, he moved next to Suzette. "Your wife? Betrothed? Companion? What is she, Bay?"

Features hardening, he looked at his closest friend, a man he cared about more than either of his two older brothers. Pinching the bridge of his nose, he let out a breath as his shoulders relaxed. Putting an arm around Suzette's waist, he met her questioning gaze.

"She's the woman I love. The woman I hope to convince to marry me a second time."

Griff clasped him on the shoulder. "Good answer. Well, I'll leave so you two can start this *courting* business."

"We're going to the Great West Café. Why don't you join us?"

"Thanks for the offer, Bay, but the two of you need time alone. Besides, I've got a hankering to eat at the Gold Dust, then mosey over to Buckie's. I'm feeling lucky tonight." His brows flickered a little on the last. Grabbing his hat, he started for the door. "I'll be staying at your house tonight, Bay. Unless you two..." His voice faded as he walked out, leaving them to figure out his meaning.

"I'll be sleeping alone tonight, Griff," Suzette yelled after him, hearing his deep chuckle a moment before the door closed.

Dropping his arm from around her waist, Bay stalked to the table, lifting the decanter before sending her a questioning look.

"Glasses are in the cabinet."

Pouring a small amount, he took a sip, then held the glass up to the light of a nearby oil lamp. "Is this the whiskey August gave you?"

"Yes, it is. Why?"

Swallowing another sip, his gaze narrowed on the remaining whiskey. The bottle at his house tasted sweet, metallic. When he thought about it, Bay realized he'd never tasted whiskey quite like what he had at home. Dismissing the uneasy feeling, his attention returned to Suzette.

"Nothing." Taking the last swallow, he set the glass down, moving to her. "Are you ready for supper?" Wrapping his arms around her, he bent down. "I've been wanting to do this since we parted." Claiming her mouth in a hungry kiss, he crushed her to him. He couldn't get over having her in his arms again, feeling her respond much as she used to, before their lives took a tragic turn.

As much as he wanted to continue, Bay refused to push her too fast. Decreasing the pressure, he raised his mouth from hers, whispering against her lips. "I don't want to stop, but if we continue, I'm going to scoop you into my arms and carry you to bed."

Glazed, languid eyes met his. "Would that be so bad?" The low, sultry voice almost melted the little resolve he had left.

"No. And yes." His eyes sparkled in amusement before sobering. "I'm not going to do anything you might regret." Grabbing her hand, he lifted it up to place a soft kiss on her palm. Feeling a shiver run through her, Bay reluctantly moved away. "Are you ready?"

Unable to form a coherent thought, she nodded. Although in her heart, Suzette wasn't quite certain if she was ready or not.

Chapter Eleven

Brodie studied the wanted poster in front of him before sliding it across his desk toward Colt. Seth sat next to him, glancing at the poster.

"He shaved his beard and trimmed his hair, and he wasn't wearing the fancy clothes he is here." Seth tapped the paper. "But I'd swear the man I met today is Ev Hunt."

"Did he give you a name?" Colt continued to study the image as if he hadn't seen it a few dozen times.

Seth smirked. "Bill Jones. Says he's a rancher from Sacramento. Rode up here on business."

Brodie rested his arms on the desk. "Did the lad say anything else?"

"No. I left him alone. He left a few minutes later. I'm telling you, Brodie, he isn't who he says he is."

"Aye, Seth. But he may not be Hunt. Do you know where he's staying?"

"Sorry, boss. I didn't see where he went after leaving the Gold Dust."

Rubbing his chin, a muscle in Brodie's jaw twitched. "If it is Hunt, he's in town for a reason."

Colt massaged the back of his neck, a cold feeling rushing through him. "And it has nothing to do with ranching or cattle."

Seth leaned the chair back on two legs, tapping his fingers on his thigh. "We need to find him. Whoever he is, I guarantee *Bill Jones* isn't a rancher from Sacramento."

Standing, Colt moved to the door. "I'll send a telegram to the sheriff in Sacramento. If he hasn't heard of Jones, maybe he can check around for us. I don't want to be accusing an honest man of anything, but I'm not willing to take a chance he's Hunt and we don't find him."

Seth joined him by the door. "I'm going to start looking for him. It's suppertime. My guess is he's at one of the restaurants, or maybe one of the saloons in town."

Pushing out of his chair, Brodie strapped on his gunbelt and grabbed his hat. "Maggie and I are to be having supper with Colin and Sarah at the Great West Café. I want to know right away if either of you lads find him."

"It's a real pleasure to have the two of you in here tonight." Tricia glanced between Bay and Suzette. "Is this a special occasion?"

Without looking at Suzette, Bay nodded. "In a way. I've asked Miss Gasnier if I may court her. To my great surprise, she agreed."

Tricia gasped, smiling down at them. "That's wonderful. Is this your first night out together?"

"It is."

"Then you must allow me to bring you a bottle of our best wine." Tricia waited for Bay's nod before returning to the back.

Suzette worried her lower lip. "Are you certain announcing what we're doing is what you want?"

Turning toward her, he lifted brow. "Are you ashamed of being seen with me, Miss Gasnier?"

Huffing out an irritated breath, she glared at him. "Of course not."

Reaching over, he rested his hand on top of hers. "What is it, Suzette?"

She didn't know how to tell him of her fears. What if he changed his mind? What if they encountered another obstacle and instead of facing it, he left again?

Shoving aside those fears, she lifted her chin, offering a weak smile. "It's nothing, really. Probably unease at being out in public after so long being alone. I haven't had supper with anyone in a very long time."

For the first time, Bay began to understand the depth of her loneliness, how she'd isolated herself because of his actions. Her one female friend, Maddy, had married Fletcher MacLaren and moved to Circle M. Prior to leaving, she'd lived in one of the bedrooms in Suzette's house, the two sharing meals on occasion.

Gaze softening, he squeezed her hand. "You aren't alone anymore, Suzette."

"For how long, Bay?"

Opening his mouth to reply, he shut it at the sound of the front door opening. Lifting his head, he glanced at her then stood, extending his hand.

"I didn't expect to see you folks in town this evening."

Colin MacLaren and Brodie shook his hand before stepping aside so Bay could kiss Sarah and Maggie on their cheeks. The whole time, the four MacLarens cast curious looks at Suzette, saying nothing.

"You all know Suzette Gasnier."

She greeted them, her voice barely above a whisper. "We haven't ordered yet. Would you care to join us?"

Colin's wife, Sarah, spoke first. "We'd love to."

Tricia approached, bringing more handwritten menus with her. "Why don't you all sit at the big table in the corner?" She nodded toward a table big enough for eight. "I'll move your wine and glasses, Bay."

A couple minutes later, the six were seated, already sipping wine. As yet, none of the MacLarens had broached the one topic Suzette dreaded. She knew their silence wouldn't last long.

Colin hadn't mentioned to anyone what he'd learned from Bay at Fletcher's wedding. The news his friend and Suzette were married, had been for several years, stunned him. Colin had made the decision to let him decide who else learned their secret.

Setting down his wine glass, Bay took Suzette's hand. "Miss Gasnier has consented to let me court her. This is our first supper together." He ignored the odd look Colin shot him, focusing his attention on the other three. Lifting her hand, he placed a kiss on her knuckles.

Sarah put a hand to her chest. "What wonderful news. You two seem, well...I don't know. Perfect for each other."

Suzette's eyes flickered, lips twitching, before her features stilled. Risking a glance at Bay, her chest tightened at the look of longing on his face.

"I happen to agree with you, Sarah." Bay took another sip of wine, setting his glass down. This time, he chanced a quick look at Colin, who'd sat back in his chair, studying him. He owed his friend an explanation, but it wouldn't come tonight.

A moment later, Tricia began setting full plates in front of them, making three trips to the kitchen. "Please let me know if you want anything else. Oh, and we have berry and custard pie."

The six tucked into their meals, no one speaking for several minutes until Colin broke the silence. He looked at Suzette.

"Has Bay shown you the property he bought from us?"

Suzette felt her face flush, remembering yesterday afternoon and all she and Bay had discussed. "We rode out there yesterday. It's beautiful with the river on one side, groups of boulders, and big stretches of pastureland. I didn't realize he'd purchased it from you."

Colin chuckled. "Not me, lass. The family made the decision."

"Aye, and it was a good decision." Brodie stuck another piece of meat into his mouth, the corners of his eyes crinkling in amusement. "It's always good to have a gunslinger as a neighbor."

"*Ex*-gunslinger," Bay corrected, his face splitting into a wide grin.

Shoving his plate away, Brodie sent an apologetic look at his wife, Maggie. "Apologies, lasses, but I need to speak with Colin and Bay."

Maggie lifted a brow, sending a mischievous glance at Sarah and Suzette. "So talk. We'll keep our mouths shut. Won't we, ladies?"

Slipping an arm over her shoulders, Brodie placed a kiss on her forehead. "I don't believe in miracles, lass."

Setting down his fork, Colin's features turned serious. "What is it you're needing to tell us, lad?"

Removing his arm from around Maggie, Brodie lowered his voice. "We've two outlaws in the area. One has a sister living not far from Circle M."

"What's her name?" Bay asked.

"Maria Delgado Smith."

Brows rising, Bay's lips twisted into a frown. "Is her brother Andrés Delgado?"

Brodie's eyes widened. "Do you know him?"

"Heard of him. He's one of the nastiest outlaws out there. I believe the man enjoys killing." Bay glanced at the women, offering a silent apology. "Delgado doesn't care if his victims are men, women, or children. He shows no mercy and no remorse. You say he has a sister?"

"Aye. Colt Dye is here looking for Delgado, plus the other outlaw. According to his information, Maria is his older sister. The lad brings the lass money almost every month. I've got a deputy posted near her farm. We're hoping to catch him the next time he visits."

"Do you need more men posted, lad?"

Brodie shook his head. "Nae, Colin. I'm not putting the family in danger. Colt and my deputies will take care of him. Assuming the lad does show up."

Bay rested his arms on the edge of the table. "Who is the second outlaw, Brodie?"

"Everett Hunt. He's also known as—"

"The Outlaw Doc." Bay blew out a quiet curse.

Brodie's eyes narrowed on him. "Tell me what you know about him, lad."

"Delgado's a worthless miscreant, but at least you know what to expect from him. Ev Hunt is different. He's a trained doctor, and although not as good as me, he's a deadly shot. Gambles, too. Not so much to earn money, but to identify the big winners. Those men become his targets. If they're lucky, he takes their money and leaves. Those who protest are pistol-whipped or lassoed and dragged behind Ev's horse until they're unconscious or dead." He shook his head, snickering. "Other times, he'll spend an entire day tending to a rancher or farmer who's been injured, showing compassion and tenderness. According to what I've heard, he's an excellent chemist. There's not much he doesn't know about killing using..." Bay's voice trailed off, a flash of understanding stalling his thoughts.

"Using what?" Brodie asked.

Blinking, Bay shook his head. "Poison. He knows a great deal about killing people with strychnine, mercury, cyanide, thallium, and arsenic." Running a hand along his jaw, he lifted a worried gaze to Brodie. "Do you believe he's in town?"

Brodie explained about the man Seth saw and what they believed to be his alias of Bill Jones. "Colt sent a telegram to the sheriff in Sacramento to see if he knows the lad, but we haven't heard back. Seth is certain Jones is Ev Hunt."

Pinching the bridge of his nose, Bay reached over, taking Suzette's hand in his. "Ev might be more dangerous than Delgado. If you need help searching—"

Brodie held up his hand, stopping whatever else Bay meant to say. "Nae, lad. I'll not be putting you in danger. If I do need help, I'll ask."

Bay gave a curt nod of understanding, his mind beginning to piece together events of the last few weeks. Tomorrow, he'd speak with Jasper and August. He had questions and hoped they'd have answers.

Then he'd take the bottle of whiskey from his house and ask either Doc Vickery or Doc Tilden to look at it. If they weren't able to come up with answers, he'd ask them to send the whiskey to a chemist in San Francisco.

A sick ache roiled through him. If his suspicions were true, the future he'd hoped for with Suzette might turn out to be a dream and nothing more.

"I had a wonderful time tonight, Bay. Thank you."

He'd grabbed Suzette's hand the instant they left the café. Even now, standing on her front stoop, Bay didn't want to let go. The knowledge Ev Hunt might be prowling the streets of Conviction had dampened his mood, forced him to think about his own history as a gunfighter.

Bay had no doubt Ev had found him after reading the article in the newspaper. He'd heard it had been republished in several bigger town papers, making it an unrealistic hope no one would come after him.

What he couldn't figure out was why Ev had come to Conviction. Although good with a six-shooter, he wasn't a gunslinger. Still, Bay didn't doubt the outlaw had showed up here because of him.

Lifting her hand, Bay kissed her knuckles, then her palm. "The pleasure was mine, sweetheart. I want to take you out again tomorrow night." He watched regret cross her face.

"You know I must return to the hotel. August gave his approval for me to hire an assistant manager for the restaurant and hotel, allowing me to return to the kitchen. He has someone arriving on tomorrow's steamboat for me to meet."

"I'll speak to August."

She shook her head. "Please don't. I want to help select the new person. After all, I'll still be the manager, even if I'm working in the kitchen most evenings." Suzette stifled a laugh when Bay's face twisted into a grimace.

"I want to see you again tomorrow."

Her brows lifted at his tone. The vehemence in his voice surprised her. "You could come here for lunch before I leave for the restaurant."

A sly grin lifted one corner of his mouth. "If I spend the night, I'd already be here and could help with breakfast and lunch."

Suzette felt her heart rate increase as an anxious jolt rolled through her stomach. "We agreed you'd give me time. I'm not at all ready for what you're proposing."

"What I'm proposing is a night making love to my wife." He saw her eyes flash, a tinge of red coloring her cheeks. "But you're right. You do need time, and it wouldn't be seemly for me to be seen going into your house and not coming out until tomorrow."

The relief mixed with disappointment surprised her. Suzette wasn't close to being ready to allow him back into her bed. Still, she remembered what it was like making love with Bay. Slow and gentle, they often took hours pleasuring each other. A shudder passed through her at the memory.

"Are you cold, sweetheart?" He placed his hands on her arms, rubbing them up and down.

"What? Oh, no, I'm fine."

A knowing grin curved his lips before he leaned down to kiss her. To her dissatisfaction, it didn't last more than a few short seconds.

"I should let you get some rest. Tomorrow will be a long day for you." Bay stroked the back of his hand over her cheek, caressing her lower lip with his thumb. "Think of me tonight."

Without another word, he turned, taking the steps down. An instant before reaching the street, he groaned, a deep, guttural sound which had Suzette hurrying to him. He'd already gripped his head in both hands, bending over at the waist.

"Bay, what is it?" She touched his arm, but he swung away, still grasping his head. "Please, tell me what is happening."

A moment later, he let out a ragged breath, dropping his hands to his sides and straightening.

The color had leached from his face. "I must have had too much wine." Given how much Suzette knew he could drink without effect, Bay realized the excuse sounded feeble. "Or perhaps I'm more tired than I thought."

She touched his arm. "I can take you over to the clinic. Doc Vickery or Doc Tilden would certainly get out of bed to check on you."

Sucking in a slow breath, he shook his head. "I'm fine now." He kissed her cheek once more before taking the last step to the street. "I'll be here at noon, if that suits."

Her worried gaze studied him, knowing he wasn't being truthful about the pain. At lunch, she'd ask more questions. "Noon is fine."

"Sleep well, sweetheart."

She watched him walk down the street, a strong sense of foreboding tugging at her heart.

Chapter Twelve

"Where's the sheriff?" Ira Greene, the manager of the telegraph office and the town postmaster, stepped inside the jail, waving a telegram in his hand. "This came first thing, Deputy. Seemed important to me."

Sam hid a grin. He'd known Ira long enough to understand almost *all* telegrams seemed important to him. "He hasn't come in yet. I'll take it, Ira." He held out his hand, taking the missive from the man's shaking hand.

"You be sure he gets it, Deputy."

Sam gave a solemn nod, indicating the importance of his task. "I will."

"I gotta get back to the office. Some foulmouthed stranger needs to get a telegram off right away."

Waiting until Ira closed the door behind him, he opened the telegram, scanning it quickly. Ira was right. This was important. It came from Nate Hollis, the sheriff in Settlers Valley and Brodie's former deputy. He'd also married Geneen MacGregor, Sarah MacLaren's sister, making him part of the family.

Standing, he slammed his hat on his head, reaching for the door when it flew open, almost hitting Sam in the face. "Good. I was coming to get you."

Brodie walked inside, Colt right behind him. "Good morning, lad." The sheriff lifted his hat, setting it on a hook.

Sam held out the telegram. "It may not be once you read this."

Brows furrowing, he took it, the frown deepening by the time he finished. He handed the message to Colt, who murmured a curse.

"Where's Seth?" Brodie asked.

"He rode out to relieve Alex. Jack is making rounds."

Brodie's jaw clenched. "Have Jack ride out to stop Alex from coming back. We'll be needing all three deputies at the Smith place."

Sam nodded, moving to the door. "Do you think the gang who robbed the stage near Settlers Valley is Delgado and his men?"

Colt answered. "Sounds like it. If so, I'd expect him to head directly to his sister's. I'll ride out with Jack. It'd be best, Brodie, if you stayed in town with Sam, just in case Delgado shows up here, or Ev Hunt pokes his head out from wherever he's hiding."

Rubbing his chin, Brodie read the telegram again. "Aye, you're right, lad. Sam, you and I'll be making rounds today. With luck, Delgado will ride straight to Maria's and we'll have one of the

137

two outlaws Colt seeks dead or locked up real
soon."

"I want this sent right away." Ev shoved the
handwritten message to Ira.

Nodding, he read through it, then began to
tap. A minute later, he looked up at the man and
quoted a price.

Tossing coins on the counter, Ev's hard gaze
held Ira's. "I'm at the hotel next to the newspaper.
I expect you to get the reply to me as soon as it
comes in."

Stepping outside, he looked around, a feral
grin tilting the corners of his mouth. Last night
had been fortuitous. He'd been on his way to
Buckie's for a few hours of cards when he spotted
Bay, Miss Gasnier, the sheriff, his wife, and
another couple at a table inside the café.

Ev had waited until they left, following Bay
and Miss Gasnier to her house. Satisfaction had
rippled through him when he'd seen Bay grip his
head with both hands, almost stumbling down
the last few steps.

A minute later, he'd dropped his hands. Ev
had heard the woman suggest they go to the
clinic, which Bay refused. They'd spoken a little
longer before he turned and walked to his house.

Ev didn't need further confirmation of Bay's condition. He'd never doubted his work the last few weeks would be effective. However, it had taken longer than anticipated.

Enjoying another rush of gratification, Ev continued down the boardwalk toward the Gold Dust. His stomach rumbled at the thought of food. Still, he couldn't keep the smile from his face.

It was time.

Bay studied the whiskey decanter in his hand. Holding it up to the light streaming through the window, he tilted the container one way, then another, hoping to spot something. To his disgust, he saw no particles, nothing to indicate anyone had tampered with the whiskey.

Setting down the decanter, he walked to the cabinet in his office to retrieve the open bottle of whiskey, surprised to see a second bottle next to it. Picking both up, he studied the liquid inside, lifting each to look at the sediment. Nothing appeared to be amiss with either. The cork of the almost empty bottle was a little askew, easy to pull out. The full bottle's cork fit snugly, as he'd expect. He didn't remember buying either one, the same as he didn't recall filling the decanter at home.

Grabbing the decanter, he took all three across the hall into August's office. His partner glanced up from a stack of papers he'd been reviewing and tugged off his glasses, lifting a brow.

"Isn't it a little early to start drinking?"

Bay didn't answer. Instead, he set the bottles on the desk and strolled to the cabinet where August kept his whiskey. Pulling out the lone bottle, he walked back to the desk, setting it beside the others. His two bottles didn't match the one in August's office. Crossing his arms, Bay glared at them, brows bunching together.

August rested his arms on the desk, his attention shifting from the bottles to Bay. "I'm certain there's a point to whatever you're doing. Please, enlighten me."

Lowering himself into a chair, he pinched the bridge of his nose. "I believe someone is trying to poison me."

"What?" August's voice boomed across the desk.

"Jasper generally buys a bottle of whiskey for each of us every couple weeks. They're always the same type, like the one I took from your cabinet." He pointed to the two he brought with him.

"These two were in my cabinet. Neither resembles yours, and I didn't buy them."

Standing, August walked out of his office, calling down the stairs. "Jasper?"

A moment later, their secretary looked up the stairwell. "Yes, sir?"

"We need you up here." Returning to his chair, August picked up his bottle, then the other two, studying all three. Setting them down, he lifted his gaze to Bay. "You can tell Jasper and me about what you believe is happening."

Appearing in the doorway, Jasper blew out an exhausted breath. "Yes, sir?"

Lips twitching in amusement, August motioned him inside. "I didn't mean for you to run up the stairs."

"It sounded urgent."

Scrubbing a hand down his face, Bay pushed aside the sudden bout of nausea. "You're right, Jasper. It is urgent."

Tilting his head, Jasper took a good look at Bay's ashen features. "Are you feeling all right?"

Letting out a shaky breath, he shook his head. "No, and that's why we're here. Do you recall how these two bottles came to be in my office?"

"Why, yes. One of your clients brought them in as a gift. Not at the same time, of course. He brought one in a few weeks ago and the other earlier this week. Why?"

"What's the client's name?"

Rubbing his temple, Jasper squeezed his eyes shut, then opened them. "Jones."

"Does he have a first name?" August asked.

Jasper shook his head. "He didn't say, sir. Mr. Jones did make an appointment but didn't arrive for it."

Sitting back in his chair, August rested his hands in his lap. "Bay believes someone is trying to poison him, Jasper." He looked at his partner. "It's time you told us the importance of the whiskey bottles."

Standing, Bay paced across the room, massaging the back of his neck before turning to face them. "Over the last few weeks, I've developed severe headaches, dizziness, stomach pain, and tingling sensations in my toes and fingers. They may be caused by something else, but all are signs of poisoning."

August narrowed his gaze on him. "Which you believe has been added to the whiskey?"

"That's my guess." Bay nodded toward the decanter. "A couple weeks ago, I ran out of whiskey at home. I planned to buy another bottle to refill the decanter, but forgot all about it." Snorting out a disgusted breath, he pursed his lips. "At least a week ago, I poured myself a drink from the decanter, completely overlooking the fact the original bottle had been empty. It took me several days before I remembered running out. That's what first had me thinking about something not being right."

"You believe someone entered your house and filled the decanter with poisoned whiskey?"

"Yes, August, I do. I also believe the same person left these bottles of whiskey with Jasper."

Putting a hand over his mouth, Jasper paled.

Bay sat back down. "It wasn't your fault. There wouldn't have been any reason for you to believe someone would offer a gift of tainted whiskey. Besides, other than my suspicions, there's no proof any of these contain poison."

August reached across the desk, picking up the decanter, studying it. "Vickery or Tilden might be able to help determine if the alcohol is laced with poison."

Jasper nodded. "If not, they could send the contents to a chemist in San Francisco."

Pushing from his chair, August walked around the desk, resting a hip against it. "Jasper, I want you to take care of getting the bottles to the clinic this morning."

"Yes, sir."

August stared into the distance, stroking his chin. "We need to find Mr. Jones. I'll go talk with Brodie. Maybe he knows something about him." He looked at Bay. "Do you have any idea who might have done this and why they're after you?"

Lips twisting, Bay nodded. "It's only a guess, August."

"We have to start somewhere."

"It could be Everett Hunt, an outlaw who's supposed to be somewhere in this area. He's also called the Outlaw Doc because of his background in medicine. Hunt is highly intelligent with an excellent knowledge of compounds."

August lifted a brow. "Such as the most effective methods of poisoning people?"

Bay nodded. "I had supper with Brodie and Colin last night. That's when I learned Hunt might be close to town."

August shook his head. "You should have one of the doctors check you."

"They won't be able to determine anything about what's happening to me until we learn what's in the whiskey."

Jaw clenching, August nodded at the bottles. "Jasper, take the bottles and go. Bay and I will be at the sheriff's office. Afterward, Bay is going to the clinic. Please let Vickery or Tilden know to expect him."

Jasper didn't look at Bay as he gathered the bottles, dashing from the office before he could object.

"Does Suzette know?"

Although it shouldn't, August's question surprised Bay. "She was with me at supper last night, so she knows about Ev Hunt. Suzette doesn't know about my illness, and I don't want to worry her until I know more."

"How are you feeling now?"

Bay grimaced. "The same as most days the last few weeks. My head is pounding, stomach hurts, and I've got a persistent tingling in my fingers. Sometimes there's a stinging sensation in my toes, but not today."

"And all of it is getting worse?"

Looking down at his shaking hands, Bay nodded. "Yes."

Suzette took the venison pie from the oven before checking the buttermilk cornbread in the iron skillet. She wanted to serve him a couple of his favorites before telling him of her decision. Afterward, she'd speak with August. By the end of next week, she expected to be on a train to San Francisco.

She'd wrestled with the decision for weeks, never expecting Bay to finally ask her about Calvan. Retelling the events of that horrible night had been difficult and more painful than she'd anticipated. His reaction hadn't been at all what she expected.

After much reflection, she guessed August had broken his silence, telling Bay what he knew. Then Griff had ridden in, and Bay heard much of it again. Those discussions, along with her adamant denial of ever betraying him, must have swayed him to listen.

When the story rushed from her lips, she'd first felt sick. Afterward, Suzette had experienced a different feeling. Relief, as if a dark cloud had been lifted and she could breathe again.

Now he wanted more. No divorce and for them to resume their roles as husband and wife. As much as she still loved Bay, the thought of going through a second marriage for show and moving in with him unsettled her. Not because she didn't love him. She loved him more than ever.

Suzette didn't have to wonder at the cause of her hesitation. She didn't trust him and didn't know if she ever could. The best solution might be to get away, find work in San Francisco and seek some much needed peace.

Her life had been a living hell since Bay left her in St. Louis. He'd broken her heart, but she'd survived, working long hours, hiding inside the house every night, pretending he might return. After a while, she accepted he never would.

Then she'd met August Fielder. He'd been visiting the owner of the restaurant where she worked, having supper with the man each night for a week. By the end of the visit, he'd sat her down, explained the partnership, the hotel and restaurant they were building, and offered her a job. When she'd inquired as to the partners, Suzette had been stunned to learn Bay was not only an investor, but worked with August in his law practice.

They'd spent another hour talking. Or rather, Suzette talked about her and Bay while August listened. She came to find out he'd already heard the story, checked it out with the doctor and sheriff, as well as a few other townsfolk who knew Suzette's circumstances. After all he'd learned, he'd still offered her the job.

She'd asked for a night to consider his offer. It had been a long night without sleep, her mind flooding with memories of happier times filled with love and the promise of a future. By morning, she'd made her decision.

August's offer had been too hard to resist. He'd given Suzette her dream job, offering a remarkable salary, which included a house. Even knowing Bay was a partner, she'd accepted.

The promise of a new start, so exciting at first, had soured within the first few days. Suzette's already empty life hadn't improved, her spirits and self-respect deteriorating each time Bay brought another woman into the restaurant.

He'd denied sleeping with any of them, and perhaps he was telling the truth. She wanted to believe he was, but how could she know? Once, she'd believed nothing could tear them apart. No matter what, they'd have each other, trust in their union, and fight for its existence. It had been a false belief.

She didn't doubt finding her with Calvan had been hard for Bay. Still, she couldn't forgive him for running, assuming her guilty without giving her a chance. Bringing women to Conviction had been done with one purpose in mind. To humiliate and hurt her. He'd been brutal in his disdain and now wanted her to forgive him and forget any of it had happened. Suzette didn't know if she ever could.

Taking the iron skillet from the stove, she scooped out the cornbread placing them in a basket. Butter and jam were already on the table, along with her best plates and silverware. She wanted to do this right, providing a meal he'd remember while explaining her reasons for leaving Conviction for San Francisco.

If she did go, it might not be forever. Perhaps she'd return one day. But it would happen when she was ready, not because Bay judged her acceptable and wanted to return to the life they'd once shared. For once, Suzette had to think of herself, choosing what would make her happy instead of what would please Bay.

Stilling at the knock on the door, she sucked in a slow breath, her chest squeezing at what she meant to do. The time had come to forge a new future, leaving the pain from her past behind.

Chapter Thirteen

Bay pushed his almost empty plate aside, sitting back on a labored breath. "When you invited me to lunch, I didn't expect you'd make two of my favorites. Both were excellent, Suzette. Thank you."

Even though they sat close to each other, he made no move to reach out and take her hand. He also hadn't kissed her when arriving earlier. His actions puzzled Suzette, made her wonder what had happened to the man who'd wanted to share her bed the night before.

What bothered her more was the sallowness of his complexion, the flat glint in his eyes, the unconscious way he lifted his finger to a temple every few minutes. Her initial decision to speak with him about her reasons for possibly leaving town fell away as she studied him.

"You're welcome, Bay. I'm glad you still had time to come over."

He blinked in surprise. "I'll always make time for you, sweetheart." The words sounded right, but the somber look on his face, the tone of his voice, troubled her. More than she wanted to admit.

"I have pie, if you're still hungry."

Holding up a hand, he shook his head. "Thank you, but not today."

They sat in silence until she couldn't handle the quiet any longer. "I should clear the table and get ready for work."

Standing, he pulled out her chair before moving out of her way. "I should be going also." Leaning down, he grabbed his plate.

"Leave it, Bay. I'll take care of them."

He hesitated a moment, then set the plate down. "If you're sure."

Giving him a half smile, she nodded. "I am." Moving past him, she headed to the door, drawing it open. When he started to walk past without touching her, she reached out, gripping his arm. "Is everything all right?"

Glancing down at his arm, he placed his hand over hers. "I've a lot on my mind. It has nothing to do with us."

Inching closer, her worried gaze studied his. "Didn't we used to say *your problems are our problems*? Tell me, Bay. What's bothering you?" Suzette didn't know why she pressed him. She might be leaving and couldn't afford to get tangled up in his troubles.

Cupping her face with his hands, he bent down, placing a soft kiss on her lips. "How long will you be at the restaurant tonight?" His voice held no hint of joy. Only worry.

"About nine."

Kissing her cheek, he stepped away. "I'll be there a little before to walk you home. We can talk then."

She cocked her head. "And you'll tell me what's wrong?"

Lips drawing into a thin line, he gave a terse nod before stroking a hand down her arm and leaving.

Suzette studied the menu for tonight, the one she'd prepared, along with the rest of the offerings for the week. She'd been excited when jotting down her ideas, ready to try new recipes.

In many ways, Trisha and Edgar had become her inspiration. They'd taken a chance putting all their savings into the Great West Café, experimenting outside the normal roast, stew, meatloaf, and steak. Those could be had at almost any town in the west.

Each week, their clientele grew. At some point, she suspected they'd need to expand. Right now, they were doing everything right, without the large investment from partners such as August, the MacLarens, and Bay. She admired them.

One day, Suzette hoped to have enough money to start her own restaurant, but that time wouldn't be soon.

"Miss Gasnier?"

She looked up to see one of the newer servers. "Yes?"

"There's a man up front. He says he has an appointment with you and Mr. Fielder."

"Thank you." Setting aside the menu, she smoothed her hands down her black shirt and walked toward the man August had brought up from Sacramento. He'd turned to look outside, his back to her.

Stopping several feet away, she studied his tall, broad frame, noticing the way his shirt pulled taut across his back. She guessed him to be well over six feet. His dark brown hair, streaked with gold, fell loose over his shoulders, something they'd have to discuss. He must have sensed her behind him because he turned, causing her to take a step back.

"Are you Miss Gasnier?" His deep, rich voice caused her throat to tighten.

"I am. You must be Mr. Clayton."

"If you don't mind, I prefer Ezekiel or Zeke. If I get the job, that is. If not, Mr. Clayton is fine."

Her mouth twitched, noticing the way his eyes sparkled with amusement. "Ezekiel is fine for now, but you must use your surname when representing the restaurant."

Mouth curling upward, he nodded. "Fair enough."

She continued to stare, fascinated by his manner and chiseled features. Sharp cheekbones, square jaw, straight nose, and the most piercing, deep gray eyes she'd ever seen. Shaking herself before he caught her staring, Suzette gestured toward a table.

"Let's sit down and talk. Would you like coffee?"

"Coffee would be appreciated. Black."

She nodded, signaling the server. They made small talk until two cups of coffee were placed before them. Less than a minute later, August entered the restaurant through the back door, heading straight for their table. Extending his hand, he smiled.

"It's nice to see you again, Ezekiel."

Standing, he took the offered hand. "Mr. Fielder. Thank you for sending me the fare to come north."

"It was my pleasure."

Suzette lifted her hand to the server, silently asking for another coffee as the men sat down. When the cup was set in front of August, he took a sip, leaning back in the chair.

"Tell me what I missed."

"Nothing, really. Mr. Clayton arrived five minutes ago and we just sat down before you arrived."

An hour later, Ezekiel walked out as the new assistant manager of the restaurant, with an opportunity to add· the hotel to his responsibilities after proving himself to the partners. August returned to his office and Suzette sipped a third cup of coffee, creating a new schedule with her as the head chef. A change she still had to disclose to the current chef.

It wouldn't surprise her if the man left, boarding the next steamship for Sacramento. The idea provided more relief than apprehension.

Sometime during their discussion with Ezekiel, she'd begun to doubt her desire to leave. Hiring an assistant manager stirred something inside her, a reminder of the obligations she wanted to fulfill. With or without Bay, she had a purpose, a reason for staying in Conviction.

Body buzzing with unanticipated excitement, she continued to jot down notes for herself, Ezekiel, and August. Without much thought, she began a separate list about Bay. Not to show him. What she wrote now would be for her eyes only.

"Miss Gasnier, we'll be opening in an hour. The chef asked to see you as soon as possible."

"Please tell him I'll be there in a couple minutes." She stared down at the last list, perhaps the most important one, deciding to work on it more at home.

Picking up her papers and empty cup, Suzette headed to the back, hearing the door open. Turning, a smile tipped her lips seeing Ezekiel walk in. Wearing a white shirt, black slacks, stylish black coat, and black string tie, he strolled toward her with a confidence she hadn't noticed an hour before. A small grin tilted her lips when she noticed his long hair had been pulled into a tidy queue.

"I hope I'm not too early, Miss Gasnier."

She appreciated his professional manner and appearance. She might be married in the legal sense, and did love Bay, but she wasn't blind to a handsome man. And Ezekiel had to be one of the most striking men she'd ever seen.

"Not too early at all. I'm going to the kitchen. I'd like you to join me." She led him to the back, pointing out areas used to prepare coffee and tea, where they kept clean plates, silverware, and napkins, and the location of various wines, liquor, and beer.

As they approached the kitchen, Suzette turned toward him, lowering her voice. "It might take time to learn to appreciate the chef's personality." She shot Ezekiel a conspiratorial look. "He's quite talented. He can also be extremely challenging. That, Ezekiel, is the only warning you'll get."

Shoving open the kitchen door, she grinned at his deep chuckle, enjoying work for the first time in weeks.

Bay grimaced, rubbing his hand over his forehead to swipe away the moisture. Between his pounding head, persistent ache in his gut, and cold sweats, he had a difficult time concentrating on the contract before him. Nor had he been able to focus on any of his work since returning from lunch with Suzette.

Even if she hadn't asked about something troubling him, he'd noticed the look of concern on her face, the way she studied him throughout the meal. It had taken all his willpower to eat as much as he had. Several times, he'd steeled himself when a sharp pain in his stomach almost bent him over. Bay didn't believe Suzette noticed, but it wouldn't be long before the symptoms increased to a point he couldn't hide them.

He thought of the discussion with August and Jasper that morning. Tonight, he'd need to have a serious talk with Suzette, let her know he might not be around to fulfill his promise of a future.

Jasper had returned from the clinic late that morning, letting Bay and August know Doc Vickery didn't have the equipment to determine the presence of poison in the bottles. The doctor did rush to the telegraph office, sending a message to a chemist in San Francisco, letting him know the bottles would be on the next stage. Afterward, Vickery packed the two whiskey bottles, deciding not to send the decanter. Giving them to Jasper to deliver to the stagecoach station in time for the early afternoon stage, Vickery sent him off with a strong message that Bay was to come to the clinic right away. They may have to wait for results from the chemist, but that didn't mean the doctor couldn't explore other possibilities for Bay's illness.

Lunch with Suzette had been difficult. He hadn't planned it to be, but whatever plagued him wouldn't let up, dragging him down both physically and mentally. Bay saw the worry in Suzette's eyes, the concern in her voice, hating himself for keeping his illness from her. That would change tonight.

If the chemist confirmed the presence of strychnine, thallium, arsenic, or some other poison, Doc Vickery should be able to provide treatment and a prediction for recovery. If nothing was found, Bay had no idea what would happen next. Judging by the way he felt today, there could be a strong likelihood he wouldn't live long enough to enjoy a future with Suzette.

Feeling his fingers tingle, Bay clenched and unclenched his hands, not getting the expected relief. Scrubbing his hands down his face, he stood and walked to the open window, hoping to clear his head.

Staring down at the street, he watched several wagons loaded with supplies pass by, riders on horseback weave between them, and townsfolk rushing across the street, doing their best not to spook the horses. A typical day in Conviction.

He turned at the knock on his office door. "Come in." A small grin lifted his lips at the sight of Brodie.

"Am I interrupting, lad?"

Bay walked to him, shaking his hand. "Not at all. Have a seat."

"I got the message from August saying you needed to talk to me. Sorry I couldn't come by earlier. Nate sent a message about a stagecoach robbery between here and Settlers Valley. There's a good possibility it could be Delgado. Colt, Seth, Alex, and Jack are watching his sister's place." He stretched out his long legs, crossing them at the ankles. "Why did you need to see me?"

Bay looked away, letting out a ragged breath before beginning. He explained his ailments, his suspicion of being poisoned, the gut instinct telling him the culprit might be Ev Hunt.

All the while, Brodie said nothing, his features a mask, taking in everything Bay said.

Finishing, Bay leaned forward, resting his arms on the edge of the desk. "Has there been any sign of him, Brodie?"

"Nae, but I've been shorthanded. The lads haven't been able to search as thoroughly as they should." Brodie pulled his legs back and stood, pacing toward the window. "What does Doc Vickery say?"

Clearing his throat, Bay grimaced. "I haven't seen him or Doc Tilden."

Throwing up his hands, Brodie glared at him. "Ach. You're as bad as my kin. Get up, lad. You're going with me to see the doc, and if you resist, I'll arrest you and drag your eejit arse there myself."

Bay found himself chuckling. The first light moment he'd had all day. "There's nothing—"

He didn't finish before Brodie took several menacing steps toward him. Holding up his hands, Bay shook his head.

"Fine. I'll go with you."

"Excellent choice, lad."

Chapter Fourteen

"Until we get the results from the chemist, I can't be certain what's wrong with you, Bay." Doctor Jonathon Vickery stepped away, pursing his lips as he let out a frustrated breath. "You have a fever, and along with the other symptoms..."

His voice faded away as he moved closer, taking another look into Bay's eyes, then listened to the beating of his heart. A moment later, he set his newly acquired stethoscope on a table by the bed.

"I'm sorry, but if you asked me to guess, I'd say you've been poisoned."

Lowering his head, Bay stared at his boots, feeling another wave of nausea. "Any idea which one?"

Leaning against the bed, Vickery stroked his chin. "I'm not an expert on poisons, but I doubt it's strychnine since you don't have muscle spasms and..." He shot Bay a wry grin, "you're still alive. The symptoms are consistent with cyanide, but it's a difficult poison to dispense without the victim knowing about it." Letting out a breath, his mouth twisted. "My choice would be arsenic. The symptoms are similar to cyanide, but it can be mixed with whiskey, wine, coffee, tea. If the killer wants it done slowly, he uses less arsenic. If the death is to be quick, he uses more."

Bay nodded, his throat constricting. "Arsenic." He glanced up, rubbing his eyes with his palms. "Is it too late to do anything about it?"

"Well, until we know for sure it's arsenic, there isn't much that can be done. Truthfully, if the chemist does identify the poison as arsenic, I don't know of any treatment, except not ingesting any more and hoping it's been discovered in time."

"Suzette Gasnier and another friend have had a couple drinks of the whiskey. Should they be concerned?"

Pulling over a chair, Vickery sat down. "My thought is, whoever did this meant for it to affect you over several weeks. They would've used small amounts of poison. A few drinks wouldn't cause more than a slight headache. Have you gotten rid of all bottles in your office and house?"

Bay shook his head. "Only the bottles and decanters with whiskey."

"You need to get rid of anything that might be tainted. Clean all glasses, plates, and silverware."

Scrubbing a hand down his face, Bay nodded again. "Anything else?"

"Don't eat or drink anything not made by you or someone you trust. I'll check my medical journals and let you know if there's more. For now, get as much rest as you can and watch what you eat or drink."

Pushing off the bed, Bay stood, holding out his hand to Vickery. "Thanks, Doc."

Grasping the outstretched hand, he offered a grim smile. "We're not planning your funeral yet."

Strapping his gunbelt around his waist before grabbing his hat, Bay walked outside. His stomach growled, indicating it was later than he thought. Glancing around, he pulled out his pocket watch. He could either go to the café or arrive early at the Feather River Restaurant so he could eat while being close to Suzette. Seeing the woman he loved won out.

Stepping off the boardwalk and into the street, he groaned at the sudden pain in his head. The discomfort had become so intense it sometimes blinded him. This evening it was more forceful than usual.

Continuing to the opposite boardwalk, he gripped the handrail, almost stumbling as he lifted his booted feet onto the wooden planks. Stopping, he glanced around, doing what he could to regain his balance. His head spun, stomach beginning to roil. Sucking in a deep breath, he removed his hat, swiping a sleeve across his forehead. Another round of cold sweats had assaulted him at the clinic, growing worse as he crossed the street.

Bay hadn't swallowed a drop of whiskey in over twenty-four hours. He'd hoped the effects would begin to fade. So far, nothing had improved. In fact, they may have gotten a little worse, but he couldn't dwell on the fact his life might slowly be seeping away.

Holding onto the rail, he continued to take slow, deep breaths until the cramps and headache lessened. He'd already agreed to speak to Suzette tonight, a dreaded conversation which had to take place, no matter how difficult.

Readjusting his hat low on his forehead, Bay continued to the next street over. Walking between Lucky's, one of the smaller saloons, and Ferguson's Harness and Saddlery, the lights of the restaurant came into view.

Getting closer, he hesitated outside, looking through the large window. A tall man with broad shoulders, hair pulled back in a queue, moved between the tables. Bay watched as he spoke to the customers, sometimes shaking hands, other times talking and laughing. He found himself searching the rest of the crowded dining room, confusion passing through him when he didn't see Suzette.

Stepping inside, Bay didn't wait for the new man to approach. Instead, he weaved his way to the back, reaching the kitchen door when a large, strong hand gripped his arm. Bracing himself for a fight, he looked up, meeting the determined, yet not unfriendly gaze of the new man.

He dropped his hand. "I'm sorry, sir, but only those who work here are allowed in the back."

Turning to face him, Bay allowed his initial irritation to fade. "What about owners?"

Eyes widening for a second, he opened his mouth to respond when the kitchen door opened, a broad smile breaking across Suzette's face.

"Mr. Donahue." She glanced between the two, stepping closer. "Have you met the new assistant manager?"

Bay shook his head. "Not formally."

Ignoring the simmering tension between the two, she made introductions, watching as they shook hands. "I should also inform you the chef quit."

Bay's lips thinned, not missing the joy showing on her face. "Does that mean you're taking over the chef's duties?"

"Yes."

Ezekiel cleared his throat. "If you'll excuse me, I need to get back to work. Nice meeting you, Mr. Donahue."

Bay gave a curt nod. "Mr. Clayton."

His face and voice softened when his gaze returned to Suzette. "Are you happy with the change?"

"I am, although the chef quitting upset the other two people in the kitchen for a bit. They're fine now." She studied him, seeing the dark circles under his eyes, his pale skin. "Have you had supper?"

"No."

She touched his arm, turning him toward the dining room. "There's a quiet table in the corner. Do you trust me to bring you something or would you like to see the menu?" She stopped next to the table.

Bending to her ear, Bay lowered his voice. "I trust you, Suzette."

Her breath hitched. "All right. I'll bring it out to you." Turning away, she stopped, glancing over her shoulder. "Would you care for wine?"

"No."

The one word had her brows drawing together. "I'll ask one of the servers to get you coffee."

Returning to the kitchen, she prepared Bay the evening's special, and knowing they were one of his favorites, added extra potatoes. Finding herself staring down at his meal, she let out a worried breath.

He'd agreed they would talk tonight. The sallowness of his features, dull glint to his eyes, and the way his body tensed every so often as if in pain told Suzette something was very wrong.

She'd thought of asking August, deciding it would be best to hear the story from Bay. Plus, going behind his back to his business partner would only cause more problems, and they had enough of them already.

"Would you like me to deliver that?" Ezekiel's voice cut into her thoughts.

"No, but thank you." She nodded at two other plates. "Those may be delivered."

Picking up the plates, he stopped a moment. "These may be the last meals of the night. The place is pretty deserted. Just the couple who ordered these and Mr. Donahue."

"Then it appears we'll be closing on time tonight."

Ezekiel didn't budge. "I've heard of him before."

"You've heard of who?"

"Bay Donahue. I used to live in Missouri, not too far from St. Louis."

She swallowed, nodding.

"Anyway, it's a name you're not likely to forget. I'd better get these out front." He pushed through the door.

His departure left Suzette wondering if there'd ever be a time Bay's past and name would fade. She also wondered about Ezekiel. Was he one of those men who'd heard about Bay moving to Conviction and wanted to take him on?

Shaking her head, she stared at the closed door. If he were, Ezekiel wouldn't have brought up Bay's past. He'd have kept silent, waiting for the best time to strike.

Suzette sat in the chair next to Bay, watching him take another bite. His movements had slowed with each passing minute. She took another sip of coffee, her attention moving to Ezekiel as he stopped next to their table.

"If you've no objection, I'll be leaving now, Miss Gasnier."

"Now is fine. You did wonderful tonight."

A slight flush touched his face. "Thank you, ma'am. Should I be here at the same time tomorrow?"

She took a quick glance at Bay, seeing him staring between her and Ezekiel. "That would be fine. Goodnight, Mr. Clayton."

"Goodnight, Miss Gasnier, Mr. Donahue."

Neither spoke for several long moments, Suzette taking sly looks at Bay while he finished a few more bites. Pushing the half-full plate away, he sat back in his chair. In the past, he'd never have left even a small amount of food behind.

Lifting his coffee cup, he studied the liquid inside before taking a sip.

"Is something wrong with the coffee?"

"No, sweetheart."

Waiting a few heartbeats, she leaned toward him, placing a hand on his arm. "Do you want to talk here or go to my house?" Suzette watched as something flickered over his face before he settled a hand over hers.

"Your house."

Standing, she picked up his plate and cup. "Give me five minutes. You can come back with me if you want."

A tight smile lifted the corners of his mouth as he stood to follow. Moving his gaze to the front window, he stopped at the sight of a man standing outside, staring at him. A rush of recognition passed through Bay. He'd seen the man before. Or on a wanted poster.

It was too dark to get a good look before the man moved on, disappearing down the boardwalk.

"Arsenic." Bay let the word hang between them. They sat next to each other on the sofa, a few inches separating them.

Face paling, Suzette lifted a hand to her chest, unable to comprehend what he'd told her. Trying to swallow the fear gripping her, she met his gaze, unable to respond.

"It's Doc Vickery's best guess, at least until he hears back from the chemist."

Closing her eyes, she forced herself to breathe, trying to sort out her thoughts.

"I don't know what this means for us, Suzette."

Eyes wide, she shot him a confused look.

Reaching out, he took her hand in his. "I might make it through this, but there's a chance I won't." He wouldn't tell her there was an excellent chance he'd ingested too much poison to recover.

Giving him a slow nod, she worried her bottom lip, inching closer to him. "All right. What can I do to help?"

Relief washed through him. Tugging her to him, he settled an arm around her shoulders. "I don't know what has and hasn't been tampered with at my place."

"Then you'll stay here."

"I don't want to impose."

Drawing away, Suzette pinned him with a hard stare. "You would *not* be imposing. Even if few people know it, you're my husband, Bay. You'll stay here until we clear out or clean anything Doc Vickery thinks might be used for poison."

The corners of his eyes crinkled in a small show of amusement. "What will people think?"

"I don't care."

He choked out a rough chuckle, his hand moving to his stomach, pressing to relieve the pain. "You cared a great deal a few days ago."

Her voice rose, taking on an urgent edge. "A few days ago, I didn't know you'd been poisoned by some maniac who's too much of a coward to face you directly."

Bay lifted a brow. "A cowardly maniac, huh?"

"What other kind of man would sneak poison into your whiskey instead of coming straight at you?"

Bay nodded, acknowledging she had a point. Cupping her face with both hands, he touched his lips to hers. Feeling her melt into him, his mouth covered hers, becoming more insistent. At first soft and caressing, the kiss became hungry, searching, setting his body aflame.

She shifted next to him, wrapping her arms around his neck, moaning when the kiss became more heated and urgent. Fingers sifting through the long hair at his nape, she let out a deep sigh. Feeling his arms slip underneath her, she gasped when he lifted and settled her on his lap.

His hands skimmed over her back, the heat of their kiss burning through her blouse to singe his fingers. Currents of desire pulsed through him

171

when she squirmed against him, the little control he had beginning to crumble.

Breaking the kiss, his lips trailed down the soft curve of her neck, settling at the hollow at the base of her throat. Using his mouth on the sensitive skin until she squirmed once more, he tightened his arms around her.

Raising his head, he nibbled at the corners of her mouth before brushing one more kiss across her lips and resting his forehead against hers.

"We have to stop, sweetheart."

Reaching up, Suzette trailed fingers down his face, her warm smile traveling over him. "You're right." Moving off his lap, she stood, straightening her blouse. "I should see to your bedroom."

"Let me help you."

Turning, she rested her hands on her hips. "When was the last time you made up a bed?" She already knew the answer. He and August hired a housekeeper to come in twice a week, a luxury Suzette couldn't afford. In St. Louis, she had been the one to clean the house and prepare most of their meals. August also had *his man*, a gentleman he'd known for years who acted as his valet and cook.

Scrunching up his face, Bay shook his head.

Chuckling, she dropped her hands to her sides. "I doubt you've ever made up a bed."

Whipping around, she headed up the stairs, hips swaying in a way Bay couldn't miss.

A grin tipped the corners of his mouth, a ball of warmth pooling in his stomach. She'd always done this to him, causing his body to react in a way no other woman could.

Settling against the sofa, his mind drifted back to the restaurant, thinking of the man he'd seen. Closing his eyes, Bay wondered why he looked so familiar. And why, when he'd first spotted him, a piercing blast of dread shot through him. The same dread he felt now. Whoever the man was, Bay knew he wasn't a friend. And he meant to cause harm.

Chapter Fifteen

Suzette stretched her arms above her head, feeling a wave of peace rush through her until she remembered Bay and the reason he slept in the bedroom next to hers. Sitting up, she threw back the covers.

Last night had been long and disturbing. It had taken hours for her to fall asleep, her mind going over all she'd learned from Bay. Coupled with her own misgivings about giving their marriage a second chance, she found herself more conflicted than ever.

As important as they were, her issues with trust would have to wait until Doc Vickery heard from the chemist. If he'd been poisoned, she wouldn't leave Bay to work through the illness alone. Once he recovered, she'd face her problems with trust whenever they were together.

With her additional role as the chef for the restaurant and hiring Ezekiel, Suzette had already made the decision to stay in Conviction, at least for a while. She loved her new job, although an assistant chef would need to be hired soon.

After one night, Ezekiel appeared to be a success. Unless something changed, and ignoring the unintended misunderstanding with Bay, he'd soon be given more responsibilities in the hotel.

Getting out of bed, she padded to the vanity, brushing her hair until it shined. Going through her ablutions, she swept her hair up, then dressed, intending to fix breakfast for the two of them.

Stepping into the hall, Suzette moved to Bay's door, softly knocking. "Bay?" When he didn't answer, she knocked once more, calling his name again. "Bay, are you awake?"

After another moment, she gripped the knob, debating an instant before turning it. With a gentle push, she stepped inside, jaw dropping. The bed was empty and appeared as if it had never been slept in. Glancing around, she saw Bay and his clothes were gone.

Unexpected disappointment gripped her, as well as a good deal of concern. She'd seem him enter the room the night before and hadn't heard him leave, even though her room was next door and she'd lain awake for hours.

Moving closer to the bed, she studied it. Touching the spread, she felt the lumps in the blanket underneath, saw the pillow had been used. A trace of a grin appeared, relieved to know he'd at least stayed for a while. Unease took over as she wondered where he'd gone at such an early hour.

Leaving the door open, she started downstairs, stopping at the sound of the front door opening. Holding her breath, she stepped back, waiting to see who appeared.

"Suzette, are you here?"

She let out a breath at Bay's voice. "I'm upstairs." Taking the stairs down, she met him near the kitchen door. "I didn't know you'd left."

Bending, he kissed her cheek, holding up the satchel in his hand, his voice still holding a measure of weariness. "I woke early and decided to pack some clothes. You don't object, do you?"

"Of course not." Although the thought of him living with her caused not a small amount of anxiety, Suzette knew making the offer was the right decision.

"I'll set this upstairs, then take you to breakfast." He started to move past her, stopping when she touched his shoulder.

"If you don't mind, Bay, I planned to cook here."

An appreciative grin lit his face. "I'd like that." He let his gaze wander over her, deriding himself for the hundredth time for leaving her behind. "May I help you?"

Crossing her arms, she lifted a brow. "I didn't know you'd learned to cook."

Shrugging, he glanced over her shoulder into the kitchen. "I haven't, but you're so good, I thought you could teach me."

The hopeful expression caught her attention. Gripping his arm, she held him still, studying his face.

"You look much better this morning. How do you feel?"

Setting down the satchel, he slid his hands up and down her arms. "Better than yesterday. For the first time in weeks, I woke up without the strong pounding in my head. It still throbs, but not as powerfully as yesterday."

Her eyes sparked with hope. "That's wonderful."

He continued rubbing her arms, voice thickening as his gaze caught hers. "I'm still suffering from stomach cramps, and my hands and feet still tingle, but nothing compared to what I've been experiencing. By staying here, I hope to improve a great deal more."

Suzette didn't have to understand his meaning. "Bay..." She let her voice trail off, glancing away.

"Don't say anything now." He let his hands skim down her arms, threading his fingers through hers. "I understand you're still struggling with me leaving without letting you explain. The decision destroyed your trust in me. If I could go back and live that day over again, I would. But I promise to do whatever I can to regain your faith in me and our marriage. Whatever you need, tell me."

Licking her lips, she felt a painful constriction in her chest. She hadn't wanted to talk about this again, but his actions weighed on her so much, Suzette didn't know if she could ever get past them. Moving away, she sat down at the dining room table, feeling as if her entire future hung on this discussion.

"It's the women, Bay. I can't just set aside all you've done since I arrived in town. I don't know if I'll ever be able to understand and forgive you."

He knelt in front of her, resting his hands on her knees. "As with St. Louis, I can't take back my reprehensible actions. They were callous and cruel, meant to hurt you. But I swear, sweetheart, I never slept with any of them. There hasn't been another woman in my bed since the first time we made love."

Tears pooled in her eyes, remembering that night. "I wish I could be angry. It would be so much easier than what I feel."

Lifting his thumb, he swiped an errant tear as it rolled down her cheek. "What *do* you feel?"

"An utter, soul-gutting emptiness." Licking her lips, she found herself trying to focus on anything except his face. "I always considered myself a strong woman. For a time after you left, I struggled. After several months, I regained my confidence and found a way to move on. When I accepted the offer from August, it seemed to be the next step in healing myself. And yes, I knew you were here, but August said I'd deal with him, having little, if any, contact with you." Letting out a shaky breath, she shook her head. "Then you began coming into the restaurant, flaunting your women. And they weren't just any women. Each one was more stunning than the last. I'd hoped one day, when I settled in and you accepted my presence, we could talk. When I saw you with the women, I realized how misplaced my hope was. You never had any intention of listening to me. All you wanted was revenge."

Standing, her voice hardened as she glared down at him. "I don't believe I'll *ever* be able to forget those nights, Bay. You showed a side of yourself I'd never imagined. If you put yourself in my place, perhaps you'll be able to experience a small amount of what you put me through."

"Suzette—"

"Please. Don't push me on this, Bay. It will take more than a few apologies and vague promises to rid my mind of all you've done."

He stood, following her into the kitchen. When she moved to a counter, he stepped behind her, not touching her the way he wanted.

"Everything you've said is true. If you'd done the same to me, I wouldn't have the strength to stay in Conviction, face you every day. You're stronger than I am, Suzette. You always have been. While you moved on, did your best to put my egregious behavior behind you, I became bitter, detesting you for what I thought you allowed Calvan to do. Hated myself for not having the courage to stay in St. Louis and confront you. Most of all, I hated myself for letting pride stop me from returning, telling you no matter what happened, I still loved you." Moving closer, he took a chance, resting his hands on her waist. "I'll always love you, Suzette. If it takes the rest of my life, I'll work to win back your trust and your love."

Suzette put away the breakfast dishes, glad Bay decided to leave for his office early. She hadn't responded to his plea to win back her trust. He may not realize it, but he'd never lost her love. It continued to beat as strong as the day they married.

She *wanted* to find a way to trust him again. Shoving the hurt aside and forgetting the past wasn't easy. In the months before Bay asked for her forgiveness and a second chance, Suzette thought she'd do anything to hear those words.

Then he'd spoken them. Until that day, she thought those words were all she needed to make herself whole again. It had been a shock to learn loving Bay, knowing he wanted her back, wasn't enough. Having his love again was wonderful. Putting her faith in him again wasn't, and she didn't know how to get it back.

Bay understood her hesitancy, knew she struggled with trust. He promised to give her as much time as she needed. A lifetime, if it took that long.

Time didn't answer her biggest question. Suzette didn't know *how* to trust him again.

She'd thought moving to San Francisco, putting distance between them, might help. It had taken hiring Ezekiel and the chef leaving to make her see distance wasn't the answer. She loved the added responsibilities at the restaurant, felt comfortable in Conviction, and liked the people.

Jinny MacLaren Covington lived next door with her husband, Sam, his son, and Sam's father. Over the months, Jinny had made numerous attempts to become friends. Suzette had avoided the overtures, not knowing how long she'd be in Conviction. She now had every intention of getting to know the delightful woman better.

Suzette knew if she left, nothing would be resolved. The only way to figure out if she and Bay could ever find their way back to each other would be to stay, force herself to face the pain, and give them a chance.

"Describe the man Seth saw." Bay sat across the desk from Brodie, rubbing his temples while staring at the wanted poster for Everett Hunt. Close, but not the man he saw outside the restaurant.

"Short brown hair, no beard, the fancy clothes are gone. He's wearing the shirt, pants, and hat of a rancher. Says he's from Sacramento, but the sheriff there hasn't heard of him and neither has anyone else he asked. Why do you want to know?"

Bay ticked off the description as Brodie spoke, giving a slow nod. "I saw him last night outside the restaurant. He stared inside for a few minutes, then left."

"You're certain it's Hunt?"

Nodding, Bay picked up the poster again, then set it down. "I'm certain the man I saw meets the description Seth gave you. If it is Hunt, then yes. I also believe he's the one who left the poisoned whiskey."

Rubbing his chin, Brodie's mouth tightened. "Why do you believe it's this lad?" He touched a finger to the wanted poster.

"I spoke to Jasper this morning, described the man I saw last night. Jasper is certain he's the man who gave him bottles of whiskey for me. They're the ones I gave to the doc."

Brodie leaned forward, his eyes narrowing. "Have you heard back from Vickery about the whiskey?"

"It's too soon. I'm hoping the chemist will send a telegram within the next few days."

A small grin touched Brodie's lips. "You're looking a wee bit better, lad."

Bay started to reply when the door slammed open. Camden and Bram MacLaren rushed inside, not acknowledging their cousin, Brodie, or Bay.

"You need to come with us, lad. There's shooting out at the Smith place."

Brodie stood and grabbed his hat, looking at Camden. "You're certain it's the Smith farm, lad?"

"Aye. Uncle Ewan sent Bram and me to check on her. You know the lass leases the place from us."

Brodie glanced at Bay, then back at Camden. "Nae, I didn't know."

Bram stepped forward. "Aye. For several months now. She's a nice enough lass, but real private."

"We'd best get going." Brodie looked at Bay. "Would you find Sam and let the lad know where I've gone?"

"I will."

Giving Bay a curt nod, Brodie left with Camden and Bram.

Pushing out of the chair, he looked down at the wanted poster once more, committing it to memory. Wasting no more time, Bay headed outside, glancing up and down the boardwalk. He needed to find Sam. Then he'd hunt down Ev.

The stagecoach rumbled along the rutted road toward Conviction, Miss Evangeline Rousseau bouncing along with each bump. It had been a long trip from her hometown of Grand Rapids, Michigan, and many years since she'd seen her childhood friend, Suzette.

She'd never considered leaving, until the death of her parents in a buggy accident left her with a good amount of money but no other family. Except for Suzette, who was more a sister than a friend.

"Five minutes to Conviction."

Her excitement grew at the shouted cry from the driver. Leaning out the window, she drew in a deep breath. The warm air worked to calm her, as did the cloudless sky and patches of wildflowers along the road.

Vangie thought of her decision to surprise Suzette. She could've sent a letter, explaining her reason to travel west. Maybe she should've. Well, nothing could be done about it now. Feeling the stagecoach slow to a stop, she felt her heart rate surge.

"Conviction." The driver jumped down, opening the door.

Scooting to the other side of the stage, Vangie accepted the offered hand, taking her first step into an unplanned future. Looking around, she moved to the boardwalk where the driver had set her two trunks and satchel.

"Ma'am." Bay took slow steps toward her, touching the brim of his hat.

She glanced at him standing a few feet away. "Yes?"

"If you're looking for help with your luggage, there are always a couple boys at the stagecoach office." He nodded at boys of about twelve walking toward them.

An appreciative smile broke across her face. "Thank you so much."

"My pleasure." He turned away, stopping when she called to him.

"Excuse me, but you didn't introduce yourself."

Turning back, he doffed his hat, making a slight bow. "My apologies. I'm Bayard Donahue."

Her mouth dropped open, the smile turning hopeful. "Would you be Suzette's husband?"

Bay cocked his head, glancing around, making certain no one overheard. "I am, although most people in town don't know about us."

Vangie recalled the last letter from Suzette. "I'm sorry you two are still having trouble, Mr. Donahue."

"Bay, please. And you would be?"

A slight flush crept up her cheeks. "Miss Evangeline Rousseau."

"Vangie?"

Her smile returned. "The same. I have to confess, Suzette doesn't know I'm coming."

Giving her a conspiratorial wink, he picked up her satchel. "Excellent. I'm certain she'll be glad to see you." He spoke with the two boys, handed them some coins, then returned to Vangie, holding out his arm. "It would be my pleasure to escort you to Suzette's house."

Chapter Sixteen

Camden and Bram followed Brodie to the spot where Colt and his deputies should be watching the Smith place. Finding no sign of them, they looked around. No tracks, no shells, nothing.

"There's a group of lads outside the house." Camden pointed ahead.

Pulling field glasses from his saddlebag, Brodie focused down the valley. "It's Colt and the others. Let's go, lads."

It didn't take long to reach where the men stood in a group, talking. At their feet lay two bodies. Colt broke away from the circle, meeting Brodie. He nodded at Camden and Bram, hitching a thumb over his shoulder.

"We almost caught him, Brodie. There were four that we saw." He nodded at the two bodies. "These two and the one who rode off with Delgado."

Brodie looked over his shoulder at the house. "Where's Mrs. Smith?"

"Inside with the children. Delgado and his men appeared while she was outside. We didn't give them time for a family reunion before we rode in from three directions."

Seth moved next to them. "Delgado herded her inside, then came straight at Alex. He fired his two six-shooters, clipping him in the shoulder."

Turning, Brodie walked to Alex, whose shirtsleeve dripped with blood. "We need to get you to town, lad."

Shaking his head, Alex glanced at his arm. "A lot of blood, but no real damage."

"I'll be inside, talking with Maria Smith." Colt took a step away.

Brodie looked at the others. "Take Seth and Jack with you."

Colt lifted a brow. "I won't be needing Jack."

One corner of Brodie's mouth tilted upward. "He's good with children."

Colt's eyes widened in understanding. "Fine. He'll come with me."

Brodie motioned to his cousins. "Cam and Bram, I'll need your help with the bodies." He walked to Jack's horse, leading the animal next to the dead men, glancing at his cousins. "Tie them down good, lads. Alex, Jack will be riding back with you." Brodie didn't mention he wanted someone with his wounded deputy in case he became dizzy from blood loss.

By the time they finished securing the bodies, Colt, Seth, and Jack emerged from the house, all three expressionless. Without asking, Brodie knew they'd learned nothing from Maria Smith.

Colt stepped in front of him. "I've never met a woman so determined to protect a murderer. She won't talk at all. Never muttered a word while we were inside. Seth searched the house, not finding a horde of cash. I don't think Delgado had time to give her the money before we rode in. That means he'll most likely come back."

A humorless grin formed on Brodie's face. "Aye."

"Here we are." Bay walked up the steps, Vangie still on his arm.

They'd engaged in small talk, nothing serious, and nothing about Suzette. If she wanted to divulge their troubles to Vangie, it would be her decision, not his.

He didn't bother to knock before opening the door and guiding her inside. "Suzette, are you home?"

"In the kitchen, Bay."

Leaving Vangie in the parlor, he continued on to the kitchen, approaching her with caution. Having so much to resolve, he didn't know what to expect.

"Hello, sweetheart."

She walked toward him, drying her hands on a towel. A smile touched her lips, although it wasn't the bright one of welcome he'd hoped to see. "I didn't expect you this afternoon."

Leaning down, he kissed her cheek, glad she didn't jerk away. "A woman came on today's stagecoach. She looked lost, so I approached, told her about the boys who deliver luggage. I believe you know her."

Brows lifting, she removed the apron. "Who?"

"Come out and see."

Eyes flashing in confusion, she nodded, following him out of the kitchen. An instant later, both women screamed, rushing toward each other.

Amusement crinkled the corners of his eyes, a slow grin appearing. "Well, I'll leave you two ladies alone." Turning to leave, he stopped when Suzette hurried to him.

"Don't go. Stay for coffee."

Shaking his head, he lifted his hands as if to ward her off. "Thank you, sweetheart, but I need to get back to the office." Bay looked at Vangie, refusing to react to the sudden pain in his stomach. "It was a pleasure, Miss Rousseau." Glancing back at Suzette, he brushed a kiss across her lips. "I'll be at the restaurant tonight when you close. Tomorrow, I'd like to escort the two of you to lunch."

Suzette looked at Vangie, who nodded. "Thank you, Bay. We'd love to have lunch with you."

Touching her arm, he leaned closer. "I'll see you later tonight."

Bay made two more tours around town, frustrated at not spotting Hunt. Leaning against the corner of a building, he pinched the bridge of his nose, his head continuing to throb. The outlaw stayed somewhere in town. He was certain of it. A hotel, boardinghouse, maybe upstairs in one of the smaller saloons.

Pulling out his pocket watch, he figured there'd be enough time to search for Hunt a little longer before meeting Suzette. The corners of his mouth slid upwards. He wondered how long the two had sat in the parlor, talking of their lives in Grand Rapids and what had happened since. Bay winced, wondering how much Vangie would learn about the way he'd treated her best friend.

Recalling all he'd done, the familiar feeling of guilt and shame ran through him. For some reason, he hated knowing Vangie would learn how he'd hurt Suzette. But he'd brought it on himself.

Pushing away from the building, his steps slowed as he walked down the boardwalk toward the saloon next to the Great West Café. Bay knew the shabby saloon rented a few rooms upstairs. He also knew Hunt would prefer something more fashionable. Still, the outlaw wasn't stupid. Ev wouldn't want to draw unwanted attention to himself by staying at the Feather River Hotel, which offered the most expensive rooms in town.

Bay walked inside, heading straight to the bartender. Five minutes later, he left, entering Lucky's Saloon. Continuing down the boardwalk, he checked every saloon, hotel, and boardinghouse on the main street. No one recognized Hunt's description.

Frustrated, he wondered if the outlaw would stay in one of the hotels in Chinatown, dismissing the idea. Then Bay remembered the new hotel next to the newspaper office, a location close to his house. The perfect place to keep watch on Bay, as well as Suzette's house three doors away.

Cursing under his breath, he made his way to the other end of town, ducking between buildings to enter the next street. His restaurant stood in front of him, the newspaper office to the right, and the new hotel next to it.

During the last hour, his headache had returned with a vengeance, along with stomach cramps, causing him to stoop over. When he'd started the day, the symptoms had decreased. As the hours passed, they'd increased until all he wanted was a hot bath and soft bed, preferably with Suzette beside him. Steadying himself against the outside wall of the building, he let out a ragged breath, knowing it could take weeks or months for her to trust him again.

Pushing from the building, he focused on the small hotel across the street. Besides Chinatown, it was the last place Hunt could be staying. If he wasn't there, Bay didn't have any idea where else to look.

Stepping inside the hotel, he glanced around the lobby in surprise. He'd watched the building go up, seen men carry furniture inside, but never saw the finished interior. It was lovely.

Carved wooden tables and chairs upholstered in beautiful tapestry graced the lobby. A young man looked up as Bay approached the front desk.

He offered a welcoming smile. "May I help you?"

"I'm looking for a friend of mine and believe he might be staying here."

"What's his name?"

Bay took a chance. "Bill Jones."

"William Jones is staying here."

"About six feet tall, slender with short brown hair?"

The clerk nodded. "Yes, that would describe him. If you'd like to go upstairs, he's in room two hundred, although I don't know if he's in right now."

"Thank you, but I'll come by tomorrow." Bay shifted away, then turned back. "I'd like to surprise him, so please don't let him know of my visit."

"Yes, sir. I'll keep your secret."

A tight smile formed on his face. Bay needed to go by the jail, tell Brodie what he'd learned, before meeting Suzette. His body ached, head throbbed, and he couldn't remember the last time he'd been so tired. Still, relief washed over him. He'd found Hunt. Now Brodie and his men would do the rest.

Suzette walked out of the kitchen for the third time since eight o'clock. Bay should've arrived by now. She wondered if he'd forgotten or gone to her house, too weary to come in tonight. Or maybe the man trying to poison him had tired of waiting and came after him directly. The instant the last thought crossed her mind, Suzette shoved it aside. If anything had happened, someone would notify August, who wouldn't hesitate to tell her.

Staring at the front door, her body sagged in relief when Bay walked inside. He came straight to her, reaching out to take her hands in his.

"Do you have time to sit with me before returning to the kitchen?"

She glanced around the dining room, seeing Ezekiel speaking to one of the two remaining couples. Both had already been served. "Yes, I have time."

He followed Suzette to the same table as the night before, pulling out a chair for her before taking his own seat.

"Have you had supper, Bay?"

Shaking his head, he pressed fingers to his forehead. "No, but I'm not hungry."

Her worried gaze moved over his face. "You're feeling worse, aren't you?"

Drawing in a breath, a slight grin tipped the corners of his mouth. "Worse than this morning, yes. I do have good news, though."

The worry faded at the way his face brightened. "What?"

He explained about searching for Hunt, finding him in the new hotel down the street. "Brodie knows and has one of the deputies posted outside. He'll be followed the moment he leaves until returning to his room. Brodie wants to be absolutely sure the man is Hunt. He also wants to know if there's anyone else involved."

"Do you think there is?"

"More than just Hunt involved?" Bay asked.

"Yes."

He rubbed his chin, expression clouding. "I don't know. There are still people who'd be happy to see me dead. I just don't know why they would hire Hunt instead of coming after me themselves. And why poison me first?"

She thought of his question, brows furrowing. "I don't understand how poisoning you would help if someone besides Hunt is after you."

Scrubbing both hands over his face, he pursed his lips before his eyes grew wide. "Unless the plan is to use the poison to weaken me."

Her brows scrunched together. "Weaken you for what reason?"

"I'm not certain, but my instincts are telling me there's a reason for the poison, and it's not to kill me."

Brodie rubbed his eyes, opening them to slits as the early morning sun shone through the thin curtains. By the time he and his men returned to town the day before, delivered the bodies to the undertaker, and made arrangements for a deputy to be posted outside the hotel, it had been almost midnight.

He'd woken Maggie and their son when he finally made it home, then stayed up another hour, getting Shaun back to sleep. It had taken him another hour to drift off.

Sitting up, he slid from the bed, doing his best not to disturb his wife. Brodie planned to check with the deputy outside the hotel before finding Bay and discussing how best to handle Hunt. He also wanted to make a list of anyone who might be looking for vengeance against his friend, the former hired gun. Brodie expected Colt to be at the jail early. He wanted Hunt as much as any of them, except possibly Bay.

Before he could leave the house, a loud pounding sounded at the front door, waking both Maggie and Shaun. Cursing under his breath, he stalked to the door. Pulling it open, his jaw dropped in surprise.

Camden sat on the ground, reeking of whiskey, a foolish grin on his face. "Ach. There you are, Brodie. I'd thought you'd never open the door."

Crossing his arms, he glared down at his cousin. "Are you daft, Cam?"

"Aye, daft I am." His head lolled to one side, eyes rolling back in his head.

"What's going on?" Maggie stepped next to Brodie, anger simmering at the sight of Camden. "Are you drunk?"

"Aye, lass. Very drunk." He slapped his thigh, chuckling. "I fell off my horse. The foul beast ran off."

Shaking his head, Brodie looked at Maggie. "We can't leave the lad outside."

She bent down to take one arm while Brodie took the other, dragging Camden inside, lifting him onto the sofa. "I'll get a blanket."

"And headache powder, lass. This miscreant is going to need it."

Camden looked up, his red eyes drooping. "I just need to find Duke and I'll be off."

"What you need is to sleep off the whiskey, lad." Brodie murmured a curse as Maggie spread the blanket over Camden. "Did you spend the entire night at Buckie's?"

Shaking his head, he tried to focus on the man hovering over him. "Nae. I slept right there." He pointed toward the door.

"Ach, lad. You could've let us know before now you were outside."

Touching his head, Camden's mouth twisted. "Nae, I couldn't." His eyes closed on the last.

Leaning down, Brodie jostled his shoulder. "Why'd you get yourself in such a fit with whiskey?"

Eyes opening to slits, his brows furrowed. "Betsy left town."

Brodie and Maggie exchanged glances. "Who's Betsy?" she asked.

Scratching his head, Camden looked up at them in confusion. "The woman I intended to marry."

Chapter Seventeen

"There's been no sign of him, Brodie." Jack shoved his hands into his pockets, glancing at the hotel entrance. "Seth watched until two this morning, then I took over. He didn't see him, either."

Massaging the back of his neck, he thought of his morning. After Camden's drunken confession, he'd closed his eyes and passed out. Thank God he had a wife with endless patience and an understanding nature. She'd sent Brodie on his way, assuring him his intoxicated cousin would be fine.

Camden being drunk didn't concern him as much as the reason for drowning himself in whiskey. Since becoming sheriff, Brodie hadn't been as close to his family as before moving to town. He'd take Maggie and Shaun out for Sunday supper, and sometimes during the week. Learning Camden had intended to marry emphasized how little he knew about what was going on at the ranch.

"I'm going inside to make sure Hunt didn't leave, Jack." Strolling inside, Brodie looked around before walking to the counter. He recognized the young man as being the son of one of the nearby ranchers.

"Good morning, Sheriff. What can I do for you?"

Scratching the stubble on his face, Brodie struggled to remember the name Hunt was using. "Is Bill Jones still at the hotel?"

"You're the second person looking for him. The other was that lawyer who works with Mr. Fielder."

Brodie's patience disappeared. He already knew about Bay stopping by. "Is he still here?"

The clerk's body jerked. "Sorry, Sheriff. No. He left before sunup this morning."

"Did the lad say where he was going?"

"No, sir. He left before I started this morning, so I didn't speak with him. Mr. Jones left a note on the counter."

"Thanks." Brodie hadn't expected him to get out of town so soon, unless he'd heard Bay had been asking about him. Stepping outside, he found Jack leaning against the side of the building. "Hunt's gone. He left early this morning. I need to let Bay know. Jack, you go back to the jail and let the lads know about Hunt."

"Do you think he took off, Sheriff?"

"Nae. I'm thinking he learned Bay found him and moved spots. I want the lads to keep looking for him."

Although his eyes crinkled at the corners, Jack's features were serious. "Yes, sir, Sheriff. You can depend on me."

Brodie grinned at the way he hurried off. No matter how much time passed or how long he'd been a deputy, Jack never changed. His excitement and dedication to the job couldn't be missed and were as much a part of him as the badge on his chest.

Walking around the side of the hotel, he headed to Bay's house. After knocking for several minutes, he gave up, deciding to try his office. Before he got too far, the front door of Suzette's house opened. Brodie hid his chuckle, seeing Bay come down the steps.

"Good morning, Sheriff."

"Bay. Seems you and your bonny lass must be getting along."

Glancing behind him at the front door, he thought of Suzette, wondering if she wanted him in her bed as much as he wanted her in his. "Suzette suggested I stay here. Since whoever added poison to my whiskey wouldn't have been inside her house, it would be safer than staying at mine. There's nothing more to it, Brodie. Are you headed to the jail?"

"I've been looking for you, lad. Hunt left the hotel early this morning."

Bay expelled a frustrated breath.

"Jack's letting the other lads know."

"You don't think he left town?" Bay asked.

"Nae. My instincts say he's still in town." He clasped Bay on the shoulder. "We'll find him, lad."

They walked in silence a few minutes before Brodie changed the subject. "Did you hear anything about Cam seeing a woman here in town? He called the lass Betsy."

Bay thought a moment, a knowing grin twisting his mouth. "I saw him a couple weeks ago in the Feather River Restaurant with a young woman. Cam introduced her as Miss Betsy Arrington. My understanding is she came out from back east to visit a cousin before traveling on to San Francisco."

"Cousin?" Brodie asked.

"Deke Arrington. He works at the saddlery with his uncle, Rube Ferguson."

"Aye, I know the lad. There was a time we thought he might court Jinny, but the lass's heart belonged to Sam. Even after he left her to go home to Baltimore, she had no interest in any other lad."

"Good thing he came back," Bay chuckled. "So Cam's interested in Deke's cousin?"

"*Was* interested. He's brooding about the lass now. I found Cam drunk as a skunk outside the front door this morning." Brodie shook his head, mouth tight. "Seems the lass left town."

"They seemed to have a good time at the restaurant, but I didn't know Cam had strong feelings for her."

"Enough to get falling down drunk after the lass left."

Bay chuckled again. "Whiskey can be real good medicine for a broken heart."

"Are you speaking from experience, lad?"

His mouth slipped into a thin line. "Long months of it."

Brodie studied him. He didn't generally get into someone else's business, but something had bothered him for a while. "Did you and Suzette know each other before the lass came here?"

"Colin didn't tell you?"

"Nae. The lad hasn't said a word to me."

They stopped next to the gunsmith shop on the main street. To the right was Bay's office, the jail to the left. Pushing his hat farther back on his forehead, he looked at Brodie.

"Suzette is my wife."

Dave Calvan signed the register at the run-down hotel in the Chinatown section of Conviction. He could afford better, but had to be careful. Bay would suspect he'd stay at one of the better places. There'd be little chance he'd search for him here.

He and two of his men had ridden to Conviction within a day of receiving Ev's telegram. The trip gave him time to consider how to kill Bay, and maybe his estranged wife. He'd been surprised to learn Suzette lived a few houses away from the husband who'd left her behind. Calvan had felt a deep satisfaction knowing the pain he'd caused both people.

Taking the offered keys to his room and the one for his men, he slung the saddlebags over a shoulder, taking the stairs to his room. The place was cramped. A single bed shoved against one wall, a dresser against another with a bowl, pitcher, and oil lamp on top. Sparse, clean, and located in a place Bay would never suspect.

Unlike in St. Louis, Calvan now had a beard and mustache, his hair longer, falling below his collar. The change would make it almost impossible for either Bay or Suzette to recognize him. At least not in time to thwart his actions.

Pocketing the two keys, he looked out the open window to the bustling street below. The smells of fish, slaughtered chickens, and unfamiliar spices filled the air, making his stomach growl. He'd made arrangements to meet Ev Hunt and his men at the Gold Dust for lunch before going to Buckie's for cards and whiskey while making plans to draw Bay out.

Heading downstairs, Calvan stepped into the afternoon sun, glancing up and down the crowded street. He'd never been to Conviction before this trip, hadn't realized how many people were packed into Chinatown. If they all lived within this small section of town, he guessed at least five or six people must live in the rooms above and behind the storefronts.

This would be the perfect place to call out Bay. His weakened condition would work in Calvan's favor, as would the likelihood the residents of this area wouldn't run for the sheriff. If they did, he doubted anyone who lived in this section spoke enough English to be understood.

Strolling down the street, he walked along the river for several minutes before turning toward the main street. He stopped a moment when he read the sign above one particular door.

Law Offices of Fielder and Donahue.

A smile as cold as ice formed on Calvan's face. Soon, there'd be one less name on the sign. One more hired gun in the ground.

After Bay gave a brief explanation of his marriage to Suzette, leaving a stunned Brodie standing on the boardwalk, he returned to his office. Speaking with Jasper a few minutes, he walked up the stairs. For a moment, Bay thought of bypassing August's office. Then he heard two voices from behind the closed door, recognizing both. Knocking, he waited until being invited inside.

"Ah, Bay. Griff and I were just speaking about you." August motioned to an empty chair.

He clasped his friend's shoulder before sitting. "I wondered where you got off to."

"I rode to Settlers Valley."

Bay lifted a brow, cocking his head.

Griff glanced at August, continuing when the older man nodded. "Nate Hollis and Blaine MacLaren are in discussions for some additional land. They're proposing a partnership."

When Bay cast August a confused glance, his partner leaned forward, clasping his hands together on the desktop. "I know you've been handling the work for the property in Settlers Valley, but I thought this would be a good time for Griff to get a taste of what we do."

Bay shifted toward his friend, eyes glinting in amusement. "Are you thinking of joining us, Griff?"

"You suggested I use my degree in law, and August asked me to consider it. I have nothing more interesting, so..." Griff shrugged, letting his voice trail off.

"Excellent decision. We do have two empty offices."

"He's already chosen the office next to you, Bay. We'll be sharing our law library and he'll be using Jasper."

Griff went on to describe his meeting with Nate and Blaine, including their idea of breeding and training horses. "They're buying land from a local rancher who's leaving to join family in Sacramento. I believe the contract can be completed within two weeks. In the meantime, I'll be looking for other clients."

August relaxed back in his chair. "We've a good number of clients. I assure you, Griff, there is plenty of work for you right now. Most of it boring, but it does pay well. I'll ask Jasper to discuss some contracts after I've gone over them. Now, I would like to invite you both to join me, Kyla MacLaren, and a few others at my house on Sunday for supper. Of course, I'll invite Suzette Gasnier." He sent a pointed look at Bay.

"I'll let her know, August. Since the restaurant is closed on Sundays, I'm certain she's free to attend." His brows furrowed. "Would you mind if she brings a friend? The woman just arrived from Michigan. Miss Evangeline Rousseau."

Griff's gaze shifted to Bay, a brow lifting.

"Certainly. Please extend an invitation to Miss Rousseau, and plan to arrive an hour after church."

After another half an hour discussing various clients, Bay suggested lunch at the Great West. August begged off, but Griff accepted, both men stepping inside the café a few minutes later. Suzette and Vangie sat at a table near the kitchen, talking quietly, unaware of the two approaching.

"May we join you, ladies?"

Bay's voice caused Suzette to sit back, the corners of her mouth sliding upward. "Bay, Griff. Yes, please do. Vangie, this is Griffen MacKenzie, a good friend. Griff, this is Miss Evangeline Rousseau."

Griff made a slight bow. "Miss Rousseau. It's a pleasure."

"It's wonderful to meet you, Mr. MacKenzie."

"Since we're both friends of Bay and Suz, I'd prefer you call me Griff."

A slight blush crept up her cheeks. "Then you must address me as Vangie."

Just as the men sat down, the door opened, Camden walking inside.

"Cam, come join us," Bay called, then looked at Suzette. "If you don't mind."

"Not at all. Good afternoon, Cam."

Taking off his hat, he grinned. "Suzette."

She introduced Griff, then Vangie, noticing how Camden's gaze lingered on her friend.

"Seems the table has grown." Tricia walked toward them, took their orders, then disappeared into the kitchen. Several minutes later, she returned, placing full plates before them.

Bay and Griff spent much of the time regaling the others with stories of their time in law school and exploits afterward, saying nothing about the marriage. Vangie asked questions, while Suzette made a few comments. Camden remained silent, occasionally glancing at Vangie as he ate.

"Are you ladies walking back home after you finish?" Bay asked.

Suzette shifted her gaze to him, feeling the familiar wave of longing. "We're going to the mercantile first."

"Good. Griff and I are on our way back to the office. We'll walk with you."

Suzette searched Bay's face, seeing lines of worry, but not the deep weariness of a few days before. He also wasn't pressing on his temples every few minutes.

"You appear to be doing much better. Has Doc Vickery heard from the chemist?"

"Not yet. I plan to go by the clinic later today."

Griff pushed his chair away from the table, pulling out bills from his pocket. "Thank you for sharing your table, ladies." He glanced to his side. "I'm sure I'll be seeing you again, Cam."

He stood, brows lifting.

"August asked me to ride to Settlers Valley to meet with Nate Hollis and Blaine."

The confusion left Camden's face, replaced by understanding. "Aye. The lads are talking of expanding the horse breeding and training we have here. When the sale is final, I'll be joining them for a time."

"Settlers Valley?" Vangie asked, looking at Camden.

"It's north of here, lass. My family owns the Circle M. We've expanded, and my cousin, Blaine, runs the property near Settlers Valley." Picking up his hat from a nearby chair, he extended his hand to Griff. "Seems we *will* be seeing each other, lad." Nodding at the others, Camden settled the hat on his head and left.

A few seconds passed before gunfire erupted outside. Bay's gaze whipped to the front window, cursing as he drew his gun. He looked at Suzette.

"Do *not* leave until I find out what's going on out there."

Holding both of his six-shooters, Griff followed him outside. They hadn't gone more than a couple feet when they spotted someone crumpled in the middle of street.

"Sonofabitch," Bay bit out, running to Camden's prone body.

Chapter Eighteen

Kneeling beside Camden, Bay muttered another oath as a bullet hit the dirt a few feet away. Holding his gun out, he scanned the street, seeing two cowboys. One held a bottle in his left hand, a gun in his right, his shots going wild, as did the bullets from the other man.

"Get the doc!" Bay yelled at no one in particular, seeing Griff rush across the street to the clinic, his gun held out in front of him. "Cam, can you hear me?"

"How's the lad?" Brodie's strained voice came from beside Bay.

"I don't know. Griff's getting the doc." Bay looked down the street, seeing Sam and Seth dragging both cowboys toward the jail.

"Cam, can you hear me, lad?" Brodie's expression went from strained to scared when his cousin showed no sign of waking. With Bay's help, they turned him over, seeing blood soaking his upper right chest near his shoulder. "Ach, the bullet didn't go through."

"Out of my way." Hugh Tilden set down his black bag, kneeling beside Camden. Less than a minute later, he grabbed his bag again. "Get him to the clinic. Be careful with his shoulder."

Sam ran up as Brodie and Bay lifted Camden. "Let me help." He took one side, protecting the wounded shoulder, Bay took the other, with Brodie and Griff each holding a leg.

A low groan escaped Camden's lips as they set him on the bed. The three stood around, not ready to leave, until Doc Tilden growled, glancing up at them. "Get out of here, boys. I'll let you know how he's doing."

"Nae, Doc. Bay and Sam can leave, but I'll be staying."

Without looking away from Camden, Hugh let out a resigned breath. "All right, Sheriff, but stay out of my way."

Giving a curt nod, he looked at Sam. "Send word to Aunt Kyla and Uncle Ewan." He mentioned Camden's mother and one of the two living elder MacLarens.

"I'll go myself, Brodie." Sam clasped his shoulder. "Cam's going to be fine." Dropping his hand, he left, closing the door behind him.

Dave Calvan, his men, and Ev Hunt heard the commotion from their table at a saloon down the street. Following the noise, they made their way along the boardwalk, stopping when they spotted the problem.

"Drunks." Calvan spat out the word, shaking his head. "Let's head back."

"Wait." Ev pointed down the street. "See the man kneeling beside the one on the ground?"

"Yeah."

"That's Bay Donahue."

Calvan's eyes widened a moment, then lowered to slits as he studied Bay. He watched as Bay and three others carried the injured man to the clinic.

"The one with the badge and black hat is Sheriff Brodie MacLaren. The other one is Deputy Sam Covington, Brodie's brother-in-law."

"Who's the fourth?" asked Calvan.

"I don't know." Ev tried to get a better look at him, without success. "Probably no one we need to worry about."

Calvan kept watching as the men walked inside the clinic. "Donahue doesn't look sick to me."

"You haven't seen him up close. Believe me, the poison is doing what we want."

Jaw clenching, he looked at Ev. "It had better."

"When are you planning to call him out?"

Calvan had been wondering the same, coming to a decision. "Tonight."

Ev's eyes flashed. "Won't work."

"Why's that?"

"He goes to the Feather River Restaurant for supper. Doesn't leave until Suzette Gasnier closes the place. Donahue walks her home and stays." Ev snickered on the last, not expecting Calvan to shove his shoulder, rocking him back on his heels.

"Listen to me, Hunt," he ground out. "If he's strong enough to bed his wife, he's strong enough for a gunfight." He hissed out a string of curses, mouth drawing into a thin line. "The poison is taking too long to work. I'm not planning on staying here long, but when I leave, Donahue will be dead, and so will his wife."

Ev didn't like Calvan's tone. "You're aren't thinking of murder, are you?"

"Worried I'll get caught?"

"No. I'm worried you'll do something stupid and I'll get caught in a problem that isn't mine. I won't be part of murder."

Shorter than Hunt by several inches, Calvan was stocky with thick muscles and a mean streak few men would cross. He'd been known to take on men bigger than Hunt and come out on top.

"You're already in this as deep as me. If I need you to finish it, you damn well better stay close and help."

Ev glared down at him. "If I don't?"

Calvan leaned closer. "The sheriff will get word someone's been poisoning Donahue, and your name will be included."

"He'll also learn who paid me to do it." Ev didn't notice Calvan's hand whip out until he choked on the hard grip around his neck.

"You'll say nothing. Remember, I know things about you any lawman out here would be happy to hear. You'd be in jail, tried, and hung before you can spit." Calvan tightened his grip before shoving Ev away. "Me and the boys are going back to the saloon. I'll get word to you when I'm ready to make my move."

Bay walked back to the Great West, his heart pounding at what had happened, sending up a prayer Camden would be all right. He hadn't known what to expect when he heard the gunshots. For a brief moment, and for reasons he couldn't explain, he'd expected Dave Calvan, not two drunken cowhands standing in the middle of the street, a hand hovering over his gun.

He stepped inside the café, Griff right behind him, coming to an abrupt stop. Suzette and Vangie were gone.

"Suzette said they were going to the mercantile before returning home. I'm going to stop by there, make sure she and Vangie are all right."

Griff nodded. "I'm with you."

The street and boardwalk were quiet, showing no signs of what had happened earlier. The drunks were in jail, probably unaware one of them might end up going to trial for shooting Camden.

The men walked into the mercantile, spotting Suzette and Vangie within seconds. They were huddled over a bolt of fabric, talking as if nothing had happened to one of their friends. The moment Suzette saw them, she hurried to Bay, gripping his arm.

"How is Cam?"

Griff walked away, heading for Vangie.

Rubbing the back of his neck, he shook his head. "Doc Tilden is getting the bullet out. If there's no infection, he should be all right."

"Thank God. I've been so worried. I wanted to go to the clinic, but Vangie thought it would be best to come here, let the doctor take care of Cam without distraction."

His features softened. She *had* been thinking of Camden, doing what she could to take her mind off him lying on a bed in the clinic. Knowing it was inappropriate in a public place, he cupped her cheek with his hand, his thumb rubbing over her bottom lip.

"I want to kiss you. If we were at home, would you let me?" He dropped his hand, not stepping away.

Pursing her lips, she tried to ignore the hunger rolling through her at his touch. He'd said *home*, as if staying in her house meant more than keeping him safe from the man trying to poison him. She found herself hoping it did.

Each day, it became more difficult to remember how they'd gotten to this place. It had taken several long talks with Vangie to accept she'd played a part in the way he reacted to seeing her with Calvan.

If she hadn't been so ashamed and afraid that night, Suzette would've met Bay's gaze, giving him some sign of her distress. Instead, she'd refused to look at him, unable to see the disgust on his face. A couple years later, she wondered if revulsion was what she would've seen. If she'd tried harder, done whatever she could to signal her anguish, perhaps things would've turned out differently.

Still, her friend recognized Suzette's fear of trusting Bay again. She also understood how much Suzette still loved her husband. And only a fool could miss the love in Bay's eyes whenever he looked at his wife. Vangie also reminded her of the fact they were still married, as neither had taken the steps necessary to end it.

Chest tightening, she whispered close to his ear. "Yes, I would let you kiss me." She stepped away when he stiffened. "Unless you were just teasing."

The wariness in her voice stung him. "Darlin', there's nothing more I want to do right now than kiss you." Bay saw the relief on her face. Reaching up, he ran the back of his hand down her cheek. "I want all of you, Suzette."

She wanted to reply, say something light to soothe the passionate tension between them, but the lump in her throat made it impossible to speak.

"I need to get back to the office, Bay." Both turned at Griff's voice.

Taking a step away, he nodded, glancing back at Suzette. "Would you like us to walk you two home?"

Ignoring the surge of disappointment, she shook her head. "We'll be fine, Bay. And, Griff, thank you for lunch. We hadn't expected it."

A grin tugged up the corners of Griff's mouth. "My pleasure, Suz."

Bay cleared his throat, catching her attention. "I'll see you at the restaurant tonight."

Suzette nodded, then watched the two men leave, feeling an unfamiliar sense of loss. She didn't know why, except she'd never been able to control the incessant craving when it came to Bay.

Bay and Griff walked several feet from the mercantile before Bay stopped. "I'm going to the clinic to see how Cam's doing."

"Don't blame you. I'll let Jasper and August know."

"Thanks, Griff."

Slipping between horses and wagons, he crossed the street, hurrying along the boardwalk. As he approached the clinic door, Bay stopped, seeing a group of riders led by Sam. Moving to the edge of the boardwalk, he waited for Ewan, Kyla, Colin, and Quinn MacLaren to dismount.

Joining Bay, Colin's voice held a hard edge. "How's my brother?" His mother, Kyla, stood at his shoulder, features stoic.

"I was just about to find out." Bay opened the door, letting the MacLarens enter before him. Sam stepped beside him, nodding before following his in-laws inside. He walked in behind Sam, feeling a little out of place.

Sam's wife, Jinny, stood with the rest of the MacLarens, speaking in a low voice. "Cam's asleep now. Doc Tilden got the bullet out. He said it was a clean wound and if there's no infection, Cam should recover fine."

Kyla stood next to her. "When can we take the lad home?"

Jinny shook her head. "He didn't say, Aunt Kyla. Brodie is in there with Cam. He's refusing to leave until the lad wakes up. I'm sure the doc will let you in."

Ewan walked to the door, knocking until Brodie opened it. "Kyla wants to see Cam."

"Aye. I've been expecting you." He stepped out of the room, allowing Kyla and Colin to enter before closing the door.

Ewan moved next to Brodie. "Did the lad say anything?"

"Nae, Da. Doc says he'll know more in a couple days. He wants Cam to stay here until then."

Pursing his lips, Ewan nodded. "Kyla will be wanting to stay. I'll get her a room at the hotel."

"Let me do that for you," Bay said. "Do you need one room, or will everyone be staying?"

"I'll be staying, lad."

"All right. Three rooms. One for Kyla, one for Ewan, and another for Colin. The keys will be at the front desk." Leaving the MacLarens to wait for more information, Bay headed for the Feather River Hotel. After he'd made the arrangements, he headed to Suzette's house.

Walking inside without knocking, he moved toward the sound of voices in the kitchen. As he got closer, he heard Suzette say his name. Bay knew he should let the women know of his presence. Instead, he hesitated.

"I do love Bay, Vangie. I'll always love him."

"But you don't trust him."

"I never doubted him before Calvan showed up." He heard Suzette let out a sigh. "If Bay had only stayed and not run. Five days he was unconscious. *Five days*, Vangie. I held his hand, never leaving for more than a few minutes, waiting for him to wake up. Then he was gone." Her voice broke on the last.

A sharp pain pierced his heart, chest squeezing to an agonizing degree. He'd hurt Suzette in so many ways, and he didn't know how to make it up her. Bay loved her more than his own life, wished he could relive those days before he left St. Louis. But he couldn't.

Unable to listen any longer, Bay crept back to the door, opening and closing it loud enough for the women to hear. This time, he called her name as he approached the kitchen.

"Suzette?"

"In here, Bay."

Letting out an unsteady breath, he stepped into the kitchen, halting at the sight of her red-rimmed eyes. "Suzette?" He moved to her, his features taut, full of concern. "What's wrong?"

Bay already knew the answer, wanted to pull her into his arms, make whatever promises she needed to relieve the pain. Instead, he waited.

Unable to look at him, she turned away. "It's nothing."

"Nothing?"

"Nothing you need to be concerned about."

He sent Vangie a questioning look.

She stared at him a moment, her eyes showing the sadness she felt for Suzette.

A moment later, Suzette turned around, forcing a grim smile. "It's time I prepare for work." She glanced at Vangie. "Why don't you stay here and keep Bay company."

Watching as Suzette walked out of the room, Vangie turned toward Bay, saying nothing. Taking a seat at the kitchen table, she stared at the folded hands in her lap.

Taking a seat across from her, Bay leaned back. "I don't know what to do."

Vangie lifted her head, staring at him. "Do about what?"

"Suzette." He pinched the bridge of his nose.

Her eyes widened for an instant, surprised at his request. Watching him, she noticed the deep lines of worry on his face, the sadness in his eyes.

"You still love her."

He nodded.

"I don't know what you want me to say."

Strumming his fingers on the table, he shook his head. "Forget I said anything, Vangie." Standing, he moved to leave.

"Wait."

Turning back to her, he let his arms hang loose at his sides. "Yes."

Standing, she walked toward him, stopping a foot away. "Just love her, Bay. Give her time and love her."

Chapter Nineteen

"I must go to the office for a while, but if you'd allow me, I'd like to escort you to a late supper." Several minutes after Suzette left for work, Bay sat across the table from Vangie, both sipping coffee. "You'll be able to see where Suzette works, join her in the kitchen if you'd like. She usually waits to have her supper until I arrive."

"That would be lovely, Bay." She tapped her fingers against the cup. "Would you have time to take me by the clinic? I'd like to find out how Mr. MacLaren is doing."

A slight smile tilted the corners of his mouth. "I'd be happy to take you there before supper." Finishing his coffee, Bay stood. "I'll be back at seven."

Heading back to his office, he let Vangie's words roll through his mind.

"Just love her, Bay. Give her time and love her."

Bay knew he could do both. He also realized there was something else Suzette needed to know about his decision to leave St. Louis. To leave her.

Walking down the boardwalk, he felt hope for the first time since Suzette agreed to give them a second chance. A second chance dependent on her ability to trust him again. Bay would make certain she never again had a reason to doubt his love or devotion.

Seeing a young couple coming toward him, struggling to contain four children, a smile crossed his face. He and Suzette had once spoken of buying a house on a few hundred acres not far from St. Louis. They'd raise several children. Three boys and three girls, if he remembered correctly.

He now owned two thousand acres. Not on the outskirts of St. Louis, but a short distance from Conviction. Bay had bought the land from the MacLarens, hoping Suzette would share it with him someday.

An architect in San Francisco had been retained to draw plans for a house. It was to be as close as Bay could remember to the one they once fantasized about between bouts of lovemaking. Two stories with a wraparound veranda on three sides, six bedrooms, and three indoor washrooms, similar to the large hotels back east.

She also wanted a big kitchen with a table large enough to accommodate eight. The formal dining room table would seat at least twelve. There'd be three fireplaces and a stove for each bedroom.

As he approached his office, Bay's good mood continued. The moment he received the plans, he'd arrange a quiet, special supper with Suzette.

He'd present the design, making any adjustments to make his wife happy. Bay prayed she didn't rip the paper to shreds.

"Bay!"

Hearing his name, he whipped around to see Seth rushing toward him.

"Come to the jail with me. I need to speak with Brodie."

"Why is that, Seth?"

"While those drunken cowhands were creating chaos, I saw Ev Hunt with a group of men."

"You're certain it was Hunt?"

Seth glanced over Bay's shoulder to see a man watching them. "Yes. Don't turn around. One of the men with Hunt is outside the gunsmith shop. Just walk with me to the jail and I'll explain everything to you and Brodie."

Giving a quick nod, Bay unconsciously touched the gun on his right side as he fell into step next to Seth. Neither spoke until they were inside the jail. Sam sat at the desk, a telegram in his hand.

"Do you know where Brodie is?" Seth asked.

Setting down the message, Sam nodded. "He's at the clinic."

Seth took a seat, motioning for Bay to take another one. All the deputies and most of the

228

townsfolk knew if Brodie wasn't around, Sam was in charge.

"I saw Ev Hunt during the shooting."

At Seth's comment, Sam straightened in the chair. "Where?"

"With a group of men outside the land office. They watched the drunks, then walked to Buckie's."

Standing, Sam grabbed his hat, adjusting his gunbelt around his waist. "You're certain it was Hunt?"

Seth nodded. "No doubt."

"Did you recognize any of the others?" Bay asked.

"No, but I was concentrating on Hunt."

"Seth, stay here while I get Brodie. Bay, are you coming with me?"

He provided his answer by standing and following Sam outside.

Both stopped for a moment, glancing up and down the street, before continuing to the clinic. Shoving the door open, they stepped inside. Brodie, Colin, and Jinny sat close to each other, looking exhausted.

"Any news?" Sam asked.

"Doc Tilden says Cam may sleep until late tonight." Brodie heard the door to the examination room open. Kyla stepped out, closed the door, and sat down next to Colin.

"The lad is still sleeping. There's no fever or infection." She let out a weary breath, resting her head against Colin's shoulder.

He wrapped an arm around her. "You should be going back to the hotel, Ma. I'll come for you if anything changes."

Straightening, Kyla shook her head. "Nae. I'll be staying here until Cam wakes up."

Bay studied the strained faces, the worry in their eyes. "I'll have supper brought over."

Jinny sent him a hollow smile. "Thank you, Bay."

He knelt beside her, taking her hands in his. "You must believe Cam will be fine. He's too contrary to do anything else."

A sad chuckle escaped her lips. "The lad is rather ornery, isn't he?"

"Quite." Bay grinned, a spark of amusement in his eyes. Standing, he looked at Brodie. "Do you have a few minutes to speak with Sam and me?"

The three stepped outside, Sam explaining what Seth had seen. "What do you want me to do, Brodie?"

"I'll speak with Colin, let the lad know about Hunt, then meet you at the jail." He looked at Bay. "Do you want to be a part of this, lad?"

"You wouldn't be able to keep me out of it."

Chuckling, Brodie's gaze narrowed. "Aye, I thought so. You'll be doing what I say."

Glancing away, Bay let out an angry breath. "Fine."

Brodie sent him a knowing look. "I'll have your word on it, lad."

"Brodie—"

"Your word, Bay."

Muttering a curse, he nodded. "You've got it."

Suzette moved through the familiar duties in the restaurant kitchen, her mind on the conversation with Vangie. Her friend's advice had always helped her sort through difficult decisions. She'd been the one person who supported Suzette's desire to move away from Grand Rapids.

Her parents were adamant in their disapproval of her longing to become a chef. She was a woman, after all, and no one had ever heard of a female running the kitchens in larger, renowned restaurants. Vangie didn't agree, encouraging Suzette to follow her dream, congratulating her when she received the telegram from St. Louis inviting her to become an assistant in the kitchen. Suzette had always been grateful for Vangie's unwavering support.

This time, her advice had been spoken in a firm, quiet voice.

"You're his wife, Suzette. Bay loves you and you love him. Don't let it slip away because you're afraid of taking a second chance. The worst would be finding he truly cannot be trusted, which I believe is a flawed concern. The best would be the life you always dreamed about with a man who worships you, children, a large home, and a job you adore. Think carefully before throwing that chance away."

Suzette hadn't been able to refute any of it. Acknowledging her only decision was to either take a chance or obtain the divorce Bay offered, she did the one thing her heart would allow. When he came into the restaurant tonight, she'd prepare their suppers, order a bottle of wine from Ezekiel, and announce her decision.

Once she'd made her choice, the hours crept by with agonizing slowness. Besides preparing meals for the patrons, she busied herself jotting down ideas for new menu items, including several suggestions from Ezekiel.

He'd proven to be invaluable. August proposed offering him the assistant manager position in the hotel, matching his position in the restaurant while doubling Ezekiel's responsibilities. After Suzette agreed to the change, August mentioned a higher wage, gaining the approval of the other partners.

She'd told Ezekiel of the change when he'd arrived that afternoon, receiving an impromptu hug in thanks. When Suzette thought of the red tinge on the big man's face, she grinned.

"Miss Gasnier?"

Turning, she faced Ezekiel. "Yes."

"Mr. Donahue just arrived. I sat him and his guest at the usual table."

Brows furrowing, she set down the soup ladle. "Guest?"

Lowering his voice so the others in the kitchen couldn't hear, he leaned closer. "A beautiful woman I've never seen in the restaurant."

A woman. Bile rose in her throat. How could he escort another woman when he knew she'd be joining him for supper? Before thinking it through, Suzette ripped off her apron, tossing it on the counter before shoving open the door to the dining room. Sucking in a deep breath, she straightened her spine, heading to what she'd begun thinking of as *their* table.

Her steps faltered when she spotted Bay, sipping wine, talking to his companion. The woman's back was to Suzette. Knowing her husband and considering Ezekiel's description, she knew the woman would be stunning.

Before her courage vanished, Suzette moved toward them, jaw clenching as she thought through what she meant to say. Stopping a few feet away, her gaze locked on Bay, waiting for him to acknowledge her presence. It took no more than a few seconds.

"Suzette." A broad smile broke across his face as he stood, moving toward her. "Are you able to join us?" The instant the words were out, Bay noticed her rigid stance, the way her face appeared pinched and strained. "Is something wrong?"

Crossing her arms, she didn't reply. Instead, she shot a terse nod at the woman. Bay glanced between the two, brows knitting in confusion before a slow grin tipped the corners of his mouth.

Putting a hand on the small of Suzette's back, Bay nudged her forward. "I hope it was all right to bring Vangie in for a late supper."

Turning in her seat, she looked up at the two of them, her eyes bright. "I do hope you can join us, Suzette."

She swallowed her anger at an assumption which almost turned disastrous. "Of course I'll join you, Vangie. I just, well...I wasn't expecting..." Her voice faltered, relief causing her shoulders to dip. She felt Bay's breath at her ear.

"I'm sorry, sweetheart. I should've let you know."

Suzette lifted her gaze to his, seeing regret and something else in his expression. Leaning into him, she forced a grin. "It's all right, Bay."

"No, it isn't."

Features softening, she pressed a hand against his chest. "Please, Bay. It *is* all right. I'll go back to the kitchen and prepare our meals. It shouldn't take too long, then I'll join you."

Vangie had read her friend's distress right away, feeling a wave of regret at not considering what Suzette would think of Bay escorting her to supper. Standing, she looked at him.

"I'll be right back."

Following Suzette into the kitchen, she touched her arm. "Please don't be angry with Bay. We should've come directly back here when we arrived to let you know I'd be joining you tonight."

Embarrassed at the blatant lack of trust she'd shown, Suzette shook her head. "I'm not angry with him, Vangie, and I couldn't be more pleased Bay invited you. It's just..."

"I know, darling, and I'm so sorry we didn't warn you. Truly, it never crossed my mind you wouldn't recognize me."

Covering her face with both hands, she groaned. "I should never have jumped to such an unflattering conclusion. It's been so long since I've seen you in such finery and how truly stunning you are."

"You must trust him, Suzette." Glancing around the kitchen, Vangie stepped up to the preparation table. "Now, what can I do to help?"

Much later, the three were still at the table, having finished one bottle of wine and part of another. Suzette fought discomfort before Vangie took her mind off the embarrassing misunderstanding with stories of the two of them when younger. Vangie insisted Suzette had orchestrated all their adventures, many of which ended with some form of punishment. Bay noticed his wife didn't protest the assertions, laughing as much as him and Vangie.

All during supper, he'd watched her, wondering how much damage he may have done by bringing her closest friend into the restaurant. Until Bay saw the angry expression, the tension in her body, he hadn't thought anything of it. He prayed the mistake didn't cost him what little progress they'd made.

"Are we ready to go home?" Suzette finished the last drop of wine, her features more serene than he'd seen them in a long time. After the initial tension faded, she enjoyed the meal and conversation the same as Bay and Vangie.

Bay stood, assisting both ladies from their chairs. Placing a hand on Suzette's back, he kissed her cheek. "It was a wonderful meal, sweetheart."

Unlike most times he'd kissed her, she smiled up at him. A real smile. One he hadn't seen in years.

The three used the back door, walking across the street to Suzette's house. Once inside, Vangie excused herself, leaving Bay and Suzette alone in the parlor.

"Would you care for coffee?"

He shook his head. "I'm fine." Standing, he moved across the room, taking a seat beside her on the settee. A few minutes passed, neither speaking. Reaching out, he settled his hand over hers and squeezed. "I am sorry about what happened tonight. If I'd thought it through..." His voice trailed off, leaving the thought unfinished.

Placing her other hand on top of his, she shoved aside the fear lodged in her throat. "Do you have time to talk?"

Studying her face, Bay's features stilled, dread rippling through him at what she might say. "I always have time to talk with you, Suzette."

"You already know I love you, Bay."

His chest tightened as the pressure increased. "And I love you."

"We've both made mistakes. Too many to count. Still..." She let out a slow breath. "Here we are."

Gaze narrowing, he nodded, wishing he knew where this conversation was going.

"The fact we're here must mean something. Don't you think, Bay?"

He shifted to face her, heart pounding in a painful rhythm. "Yes, sweetheart. I do think it means something."

Fighting the part of her that warned to stay silent, she leaned forward, letting her lips touch his. He responded, cupping her face in his hands, dropping them as she pulled away. When she licked her lips, a slight groan rumbled in his chest.

"I've been thinking a lot about us."

Bay cocked a brow, unease settling in his stomach. "And?"

Biting her lower lip, she surged ahead before her courage dissolved. "I think we should get married."

Chapter Twenty

Suzette's words stunned Bay. He'd been prepared for the worst, such as her deciding she'd never trust him enough to continue their marriage.

It had surprised him when she hadn't questioned his assertion he'd never bedded any of the women she'd seen him with. Most people assumed he had, but Suzette accepted the claim without asking any questions. Bay had seen it as an act of trust. His actions humiliated her, but weren't the real reason she'd finally succumbed to his insistence on a divorce. A divorce he'd talked her out of...at least temporarily.

The disillusionment occurred because he'd abandoned her. He hadn't left a note or sent a telegram explaining his reasons for leaving. Bay hadn't communicated with her at all after riding out of St. Louis.

Although he'd thought about her every hour of each day, going back hadn't been something he seriously considered. As time passed, shoving the guilt aside had been easier than facing the loathing he'd see if he returned.

Bay now realized ignoring the pull to go back had been the actions of a coward. Admitting the weakness galled him. He'd always believed himself to be strong, able to face any adversary, never accepting defeat. Weakness had never been a description that applied to him.

Over the last few weeks, Bay had swallowed his pride, realizing those words did describe him. Cowardly and weak.

None of it mattered now. Suzette wanted to stay married. Moving before she could protest, Bay slid his arms under her, lifting her onto his lap and kissing her. Not a slow, tender kiss. This one was hungry, powerful, almost brutal in its intensity. Feeling her arms wrap around him, he tightened his hold, wanting to continue, knowing there were still things needing to be said.

On a reluctant groan, he pulled back. "Are you certain, Suzette?"

Glazed eyes moved over his face, her mouth curving into a soft smile. "I'm certain I won't feel any different in another week, or month, or year. I've loved you for such a long time, Bay."

"But what I did—"

Placing a finger over his lips, she silenced him. "Both of us made mistakes. We're older now, and I'd hope a little wiser." Cupping his face, she brushed a kiss over his mouth. "If you can forgive me, I can do no less than forgive you."

"For all of it?"

Suzette knew he meant not only the women, but abandoning her, leaving her with little money and an uncertain future. "I learned a couple valuable lessons when you left. First, I will never be without money of my own." She saw him flinch, as if he'd been slapped. "Second, I no longer expect our marriage to be free of pain."

His eyes widened before he drew a finger down her cheek. "You were always so naïve and trusting. I hate the fact I'm the one who stole them away from you."

"In a way, what you did helped me. I'd believed our marriage to be a fantasy of devotion and patience during the most difficult times. It was hard to accept, but I now realize few couples are bestowed such wonderful gifts. We love and respect each other. I'll not expect anything more."

Bay felt his heart thud, stomach tighten at her words. "In other words, you don't believe I'll stay around if we face more struggles."

Nodding, she slipped off his lap and stood. "I'm sorry, Bay, but it's the only way to protect myself."

His jaw tightened. He didn't want her to ever doubt him again, yet he'd done nothing to give her reason to believe otherwise. "Don't expect much and you won't be disappointed."

"Yes."

"I see." The painful part was he *did* understand. Standing, he took her hands in his. "Then I'll spend the rest of my days proving I'm the devoted husband you deserve." Lifting her hands, he kissed the palms of each, hearing her sharp intake of breath. "Tomorrow, we'll arrange a public announcement of our wedding plans."

"Our wedding plans?" Breath hitching, she stared down at their joined hands.

A knowing smile appeared. "I'll speak to the reverend about marrying us on Saturday. Now that you've made your decision, I'm not waiting longer than we must." Bending, hearing a squeak of delight, Bay swept her into his arms. "And I'm not waiting another minute before making love to you."

Carrying her up the stairs, he shoved the door open with his shoulder, capturing her mouth with his. Kicking the door closed, he took the few steps to her bed, never breaking contact.

Laying her down, he stared at her, allowing himself to calm, refusing to rush their first time in years. Removing his gunbelt and boots, he stretched out beside her, rough fingers loosening the buttons of her blouse while peppering her face with kisses.

"You're more beautiful now than when we first met." Slipping the blouse over her shoulders, leaving her in a thin chemise, he sucked in a ragged breath. "And you're still mine."

"Today?" Vangie set down her cup of coffee, her gaze moving between Bay and Suzette. She'd heard them the night before, the occasional groan or muffled cry. The sounds didn't bother her. After all Bay had put her through, Suzette deserved to find happiness, and if it was with him, Vangie wouldn't voice her misgivings. But remarrying him?

Bay stood next to Suzette, who sat on a chair in the parlor. Resting a hand on her shoulder, he nodded. "I spoke to the reverend right after sunup. He can remarry us this afternoon in the church."

"Does he know the circumstances?" Vangie asked.

"Bay told him enough, so the reverend understands why we want to confirm our marriage vows," Suzette answered. "To everyone except those at the wedding, this will be our one and only ceremony."

Vangie slid to the edge of the chair. "Who else will be there?"

"Brodie, Sam, and their wives. August rode out to the MacLaren ranch to let the others know about the wedding." Bay grinned. "Although everyone who'll be there already knows the truth."

Vangie stood. "We need a cake, and coffee, and flowers, and..." Her voice trailed off as she tapped fingers against her mouth.

"The pastry chef at the restaurant is baking a cake and will provide coffee. As far as flowers..." Suzette glanced up at Bay.

Vangie spoke before he responded. "I'll find some." Turning to leave, she whirled back around. "What time is the ceremony?"

"Four o'clock. Afterward, everyone is invited to the restaurant for supper and cake." Bay tightened his grip on Suzette's shoulder.

"And you're going to stand with me, Vangie. Griff will stand with Bay."

Joy brightened Vangie's face. "I'd love to stand by you, Suzette."

Both watched as she hurried out of the room and up the stairs. Moving in front of the chair, he took Suzette's hand, drawing her up to face him. Placing a soft, warm kiss on her lips, he fought the urge to wrap his arms around her. Bay reminded himself they'd have their entire lives to get to know each other again. A knowing grin tipped the corners of his mouth, recalling their hours alone last night.

"Come with me." He tugged her toward the front door.

She pulled until he stopped. "Where are we going?"

"To buy my bride a dress." He watched as her face flushed.

"Don't you think it's frivolous to spend our money on a marriage we're only having to fend off the town busybodies?"

He turned her to face him, unable to express the depth of his love for this one woman. "I'm buying my woman a special dress so we'll always remember this day."

Soft, emerald green eyes locked on his. "I won't need a new dress to remember today. We used a justice of the peace for our first marriage. He found the two witnesses, and the ceremony was held at the jail since the saloon was full of drunks." Kissing his cheek, she grinned. "This time we'll be in a church with a real minister. Vangie and Griff will be standing with us, and there'll be a celebration." The grin turned into a bright smile. "And we'll have cake."

With each revelation, his gut twisted. Suzette had never complained about how they'd married in St. Louis by an indifferent judge and witnesses they'd never met until the ceremony. Bay wondered why he'd never asked what she wanted. In his eagerness to get a ring on her finger, he'd taken the easiest and fastest way to make her his wife.

While lying in each other's arms that morning, she'd asked about a church wedding and a celebration at the restaurant. Thinking it had to do with her desire to make a statement to the town, he'd agreed. Until now, it hadn't occurred to him how much Suzette wanted a marriage creating memories she could carry into old age. Remembrances to share with their children.

Our children.

"All the more reason for you to wear a very special dress you can pack away for our daughters." He kissed the tip of her nose. "No more arguments. It's a purchase I want to make. One you'll accept with your usual grace."

A wave of sadness washed over her features before she shoved it aside. Her parents hadn't been at their first wedding and wouldn't be at this one. They'd never sent a letter congratulating them. Never asked any questions about the man their only daughter had fallen in love with and married. They also had no idea what happened in St. Louis, for which Suzette would always be grateful.

Bay was right about one thing. Her parents had been consistent in their instructions on etiquette. Learning to be graceful *and* gracious were two of her mother's favorite lessons. Suzette had learned them well.

The corners of her mouth slid upward. "If you're generous enough to offer a new dress, I'm gracious enough to accept it."

Tightening his grip on her hand, Bay walked outside toward a new store opened recently by a young widow from Sacramento. Suzette recognized it as the new millinery and dressmaker shop.

He stopped outside. "Have you had a chance to go inside?"

"Not yet." Suzette's gaze wandered over the dresses, hats, and accessories in the window. "Have you met the owner?"

"I have. She moved up here from Sacramento." Feeling her tense beside him, he turned to face her. "Mrs. Cynthia Abbott is a widow with a young son." He waited for that to settle in before turning back to the window. "Over the last weeks, she's been working long hours. Two days ago, she finished the front display and opened. Are you ready to go inside and meet her?"

Nodding, Suzette allowed him to lead her inside, steps faltering at the first sight of the owner. Slim with dark brown hair and clear green eyes, the widow was stunning beyond anything Suzette had expected. And young. Quite young judging by her clear complexion, void of any creases. The appreciative smile the woman flashed at Bay made her stomach clench.

"Mrs. Abbott, may I introduce my fiancée, Suzette Gasnier."

The smile faded a slight bit when the proprietress turned her attention to Suzette. "Miss Gasnier, it's a pleasure." Her gaze quickly returned to Bay before Suzette could reply. "Congratulations to you both. I didn't realize you were engaged, Mr. Donahue."

He stared at her a moment, as if seeing the interest in her eyes for the first time. Bay's voice lowered to a soothing sound. "Miss Gasnier and I have known each other a long time. We first met in St. Louis. I'm honored to admit she finally accepted my proposal of marriage." Placing a proprietary hand on the small of Suzette's back, he bent, kissing her temple. "The fact is, we're marrying this afternoon and Miss Gasnier requires a gown. Do you have something elegant that will suit her?"

"I'm certain I do." Cynthia glanced around the room before moving to a wardrobe against one wall. Opening the door, she sifted through the contents, glancing over her shoulder. "There's a lovely blue silk, and another in green. Either would suit your coloring." Pulling each out, she lifted them for Suzette to inspect.

"The blue one," she and Bay commented at the same time, smiling at each other.

"She'll need a veil to match." He took the gown from Cynthia's hand, holding it in front of Suzette.

Cynthia studied the lines of the dress. "It will certainly require some alterations. What time is the ceremony?"

"Four o'clock." Suzette shot a quick glance at Bay. "I'll need the dress and veil no later than three."

"Then we have no time to waste." Checking the pockets of her smock for pins and measuring tape, she motioned toward a curtained area. "Miss Gasnier, please change back there. Mr. Donahue, you may wait or come back in thirty minutes."

Moving to a wooden chair across the room, he picked it up, setting it close to the changing area. "I'll wait."

Chapter Twenty-One

Dave Calvan rested a shoulder against the outside wall of a saloon two doors away from the millinery and dress shop. Next to him stood Ev Hunt, a smirk improving his normal dour expression. They'd been searching for Bay, stepping into the shadows when Calvan spotted him and Suzette staring into the front window of the store. A moment later, the couple walked inside.

Calvan had decided the time had come to flush his brother's murderer out into the open. While playing cards at Buckie's, he and his men had overheard players at another table conversing about events around town. Their attention had risen at the news a local doctor received word from a chemist in San Francisco regarding the contents of a couple bottles. Rumor was they contained arsenic.

The news angered Calvan, but was all he needed to make a final decision. Bay had somehow guessed his symptoms were brought on by something other than illness. The gunslinger had suspected something amiss, enough to ask the local doctor to send the whiskey away for assessment. The answer had been one simple word. Arsenic.

The hope of Bay ingesting enough poison-laced whiskey to affect his reaction time evaporated at the news. Refusing to forget the way Donahue had gunned down his brother, Calvan made plans to draw him out, even if it meant murdering the well-known attorney.

He, his two men, and Hunt would pick the right time, preferably at night, and force Bay's hand. Once dead, they'd ride south, disappearing across the Mexican border.

"What do you think they're about?" Hunt asked, nodding toward the dress shop.

Calvan shrugged. "She's his wife. It appears they've settled their differences after my interference in their lives." He snorted at the last, knowing his actions had destroyed their marriage. Their pain wasn't enough for Calvan. He wanted to ruin Bay completely, removing him from the earth the same as the gunman had done to Calvan's kin.

Consequences no longer mattered. He wanted revenge, needed the hunt to be over and done.

"He's living in her house, so I'd say you're correct they've resolved their differences, perhaps deciding to continue their marriage." Hunt rubbed his chin, then crossed his arms. "It will make it more difficult to get him alone at night."

Seeing Bay and Suzette leave the shop, both men stepped back into the shadows. Their gazes trailed the couple down a narrow path to the main street before Calvan and Hunt began to follow. Staying a good distance behind, they paused a couple times when Bay glanced over his shoulder, stopping when he escorted Suzette into the mercantile.

Once the door closed, the two men walked to the front window. Bay spoke to the proprietor, Clarence Maloney, who walked to the back room, returning with a tray a few minutes later. Setting it on the counter, he pointed to various items while Suzette and Bay bent over the display. When she touched one, Maloney picked it up, slipping it onto her finger. Calvan chuckled.

"I do believe Donahue is buying a wedding band to replace the one I removed from her finger in St. Louis. Interesting."

Shaking his head, Hunt sneered at Calvan, anger tinging his voice. "Why are we here? Watching them select a dress and pick out a ring is a waste of time. We should be figuring out how to kill Donahue and ride out without MacLaren or his deputies following."

Calvan's condescending glare caused Hunt to stiffen. "I already have an idea of what we'll do."

Hunt lifted a brow, nostrils flaring. "Why haven't you explained it to me?"

Calvan moved to within inches of Hunt. "You'll learn about the plan when I'm ready to disclose it." He glanced inside, seeing Bay and Suzette turning toward the door. "We need to get out of here."

Cursing wildly, Hunt followed Calvan between a couple buildings, heading back to their hotel in Chinatown. Once inside his room, he had a decision to make, one that wouldn't include Calvan or his men.

Hunt didn't know what the crazed outlaw had in mind for Bay, and didn't plan to stay around to find out. If Calvan thought he could best the lawyer turned gunslinger a second time, he was more delusional than Hunt believed him to be.

The Outlaw Doc had worked alone too long to be drawn into a fight not of his making. Setting Bay up for a one-sided gunfight didn't bother him. It was the man's own fault if he allowed himself to be duped so easily by pouring copious amounts of arsenic-tainted whiskey down his throat. But Hunt knew Bay was no one's fool. He'd learned of the poison and would slowly recuperate.

The gunslinger would be vigilant, watching for any sign of a threat to him or Suzette. Donahue might even suspect Calvan of being the person behind the poisoning. Then again, from his years as a gun for hire, Bay had many enemies.

The danger could come from any of a dozen men who'd celebrate his demise.

Pulling his belongings from a drawer, Hunt stuffed them into saddlebags before taking a quick glance around the sparse room. Getting out of Conviction without Calvan knowing had become a priority.

Slinging the saddlebags over a shoulder, he opened the door. The hall was empty, and no voices came from the adjoining rooms. Leaving in the middle of the day didn't appeal to him. Still, getting away from Calvan and his men had become critical.

Taking the stairs with slow determination, he glanced around a lobby boasting of little furniture and not a single person. Stepping outside onto the slanting boardwalk, he took three steps before a shout from behind stalled his movement.

"Hunt. Drop the saddlebags and raise your hands." Colt Dye moved toward the outlaw, six-shooter leveled at the man's back, spitting out the next words. "Do it now."

Taking a couple steps closer, Colt's jaw tightened, ignoring the slight wave of dread always present when pursuing a wanted man. Unlike most, they had nothing to lose by putting up a fight, which could lead to death. Maybe even their own.

Seeing the saddlebags slip off Hunt's shoulder, Colt tightened his grip on the gun when they hit the boardwalk with a thud. His vigilance was rewarded when Hunt drew his gun, spinning and propelling himself toward the street at the same time.

Colt fired, nicking Hunt's right arm. Landing on the wound, the outlaw spewed out a string of curses, trying to lift the gun with his injured arm. Before he could recover, Colt stood over him, his revolver aimed at Hunt's chest.

"Drop the gun." Colt kicked it from Hunt's hand before the outlaw could react.

"Who do you have?" Bay stopped next to them, his gun drawn.

"Ev Hunt."

Bay's eyes widened, then narrowed, his gaze studying the man lying prone on the ground.

"Who is Ev Hunt?"

Bay glanced behind him, not realizing Suzette stood a few feet away. Hearing the gunshots, he'd shoved her inside the protection of a shop before hurrying down the street to see Colt holding a gun on the outlaw.

Bay settled an arm over her shoulders, turning her away from the injured man. "An outlaw Colt has been chasing."

"Does he have anything to do with the poisoning of your whiskey?" Suzette glared over her shoulder at the man, feeling no sympathy for the gunshot wound.

Bay dropped his arm, moving next to Colt. "I'll help you get him to the jail. Then I'd like to bring Jasper over to look at Hunt. He may be the man responsible for slipping arsenic into my whiskey."

Placing a hand on Bay's arm, Suzette glanced behind her, not noticing the three men hidden inside the lobby of the small Chinese hotel. "You help Colt. I'll get Jasper and bring him to the jail."

Before Bay could protest, Suzette lifted her skirts, hurrying toward his law office. Muttering an oath, knowing he had to help Colt, he turned back to glare at Hunt. "Are you the one who put arsenic in my bottles of whiskey?"

Shifting enough to see Bay, a smirk appeared on Ev's face. "Don't know what you're talking about."

Bay lifted a brow. "You sure of that? My understanding is you've got considerable knowledge about most poisons. What they do, how to use them, which ones kill slowly and which are quicker. After all, you trained to be a doctor."

Colt stood aside, noticing Hunt's eyes flicker as Bay spoke. "Let's get him to the jail. A few days in a cell might help his memory."

"You don't have any reason to arrest me."

Reaching into a pocket, Colt drew out a folded piece of paper. "This tells me differently." He held it out for Hunt to see the image on the wanted poster. "You have a twin?"

Nostrils flaring, Ev didn't respond as he turned his head away.

Colt grabbed his left shoulder while Bay grabbed the right, ignoring the shout of pain as they pulled him to his feet. Marching him toward the jail, they were careful to watch for any others who might be part of his gang.

"Where are your boys, Hunt?"

Ev shot Colt a savage glare. "I'm traveling alone."

Ignoring the stares of those on the boardwalk, Colt continued to pepper the outlaw with questions, knowing he'd get lies or no answer at all. Reaching the jail, Bay pushed open the door, dragging Hunt inside when he dug in his heels.

"Brodie, you in the back?" Colt shoved the door closed. When he didn't answer, Bay grabbed the keys to the cells. Pushing Hunt onto the cot, Bay locked the door, stopping to study the outlaw. "Do you mind getting one of the doctors to take care of his wound?"

Handing Colt the keys, Bay left, glad to put space between him and the man who'd tried to kill him. But why?

Bay had never been hired to bring Hunt in. They'd never faced off against each other. He knew the outlaw by reputation, his background as a doctor and propensity to kill only when he had no other choice. If what he knew of Hunt was true, why would he come after Bay?

In a flash of understanding, he knew the answer. Someone had hired Ev. He needed to discover who and if they were riding to Conviction. Or if they were already here.

Returning to the jail with Doc Tilden, he spotted Brodie next to Colt, then frowned. Suzette and Jasper should've been here by now.

Tilden didn't take long tending to the wound, Hunt saying nothing the entire time. As time passed, Bay continued to worry about Suzette's absence.

"I'm heading to my office."

Colt looked at him. "You going to find Suzette and Jasper?"

"That's my intention."

The closer Bay got to the office with no sign of either of them, the tighter his chest squeezed, the ball of dread in his gut increasing. It had been close to an hour. Much too long when the office was less than five minutes from the jail.

Finding the front desk empty, he bounded up the stairs, heading to August's office. "Have you seen Jasper or Suzette?"

Setting down the pen, he looked up at Bay. "They left to find you."

The knot of dread moved to his throat. "How long ago?"

"Maybe thirty minutes. Could've been..." His voice trailed off when Bay dashed back downstairs to step outside. Joining him, August's brows furrowed. "What's going on?"

Bay looked up and down the street, not spotting them. "They never arrived at the jail."

"Jasper was about to get his lunch. Maybe Suzette—"

"No," Bay cut him off. "Colt arrested Ev Hunt. We need Jasper to identify him as the person who brought the poisoned whiskey to the office. She wouldn't have gone anywhere before heading to the jail."

"Do you believe someone took them?"

Settling fisted hands on his hips, his jaw clenched. "I don't know what to think."

"Mr. Donahue?"

Bay and August turned, seeing a boy of about thirteen approaching. "I'm Bay Donahue."

Holding out a piece of paper, the boy looked uneasy, ready to bolt at any moment. "This is for you." Handing it to him, he tried to move away before August gripped his shoulder, waiting as Bay read the message.

Fiery eyes glared at the boy. "Who gave this to you?"

Cringing at the harsh tone, he tried to wrench himself from August's tight hold.

Moving closer, Bay leaned down to within a few inches of the boy's face. "Who gave this to you?"

Shaking his head, the boy glanced behind him, then back at Bay and August. "I don't know his name. He asked me to deliver the message and gave me money to do it."

"Just one man?" August asked.

"That's all I saw."

"Where did you see him?" Bay pressed.

"Chinatown."

Chapter Twenty-Two

August let the boy go, taking the paper from Bay's shaking hand. Reading it, he cursed. "We need to get Brodie."

Bay shook his head. "You go for Brodie. I'm going to Chinatown."

"They won't be there. Not after sending this message and telling you to wait until there's a second message. Who knows what they'll do to Suzette and Jasper if you try to find them now."

"Damn it, August. I can't stand around waiting. I need to go after them."

"What you need is to calm down and show Brodie the message. Besides, Ev Hunt may know where they're hiding."

Although Bay didn't like it, August made sense. "Fine." He didn't glance behind him, already knowing August would follow. Rushing into the jail, he ignored the surprised faces, handing the paper to Brodie. Without looking at Bay, Brodie stalked to Ev's cell.

"We've a problem and you're going to help us solve it." He held the paper between the bars. A long moment passed before Ev stood and took the message.

"I don't know anything about this."

Bay stepped forward. "Who are you working for?"

"What makes you think I'm working for someone?"

Crossing his arms, Bay's hard gaze bored into the outlaw. "You and I have no history, Hunt. There's no reason for you to try to poison me unless you've been hired to do it. Now, who hired you and is he in Conviction?"

Ev moved closer to the bars. "Who I work for is none of your business, Donahue."

Brodie replied first. "It damn well will be if anything happens to Suzette or Jasper. I'll be making sure you pay for all you've done, including any harm to the lass and lad who disappeared."

Turning, Ev lowered himself onto the cot, resting his back against the wall. "I don't know anything about a kidnapping or who took your people." Shifting, he lay down, careful of his injured right arm.

"How long until the circuit judge arrives, Brodie?" Colt asked.

"Three, maybe four weeks is my guess."

"Probably be a lot easier to take him to the Marshal in San Francisco. They won't waste any time with the trial and hanging Hunt." Colt glanced from Brodie to the prisoner, seeing Hunt's unsettling gaze locked on him. "I might need the help of one of your deputies, if you can spare anyone."

"Aye, I can spare one. The sooner you get started, the sooner the lad will be hanging for his crimes." Everyone knew how hard the San Francisco judges and juries were on those who broke the law. They'd show no mercy to a man as infamous as Everett Hunt.

"Wait." Hunt shoved off the cot, wincing at the pain in his arm. "I'd rather be tried here."

"It's a shame you don't get a say, lad." Brodie turned his back on the cell, stopping at Hunt's next words.

"I might know where they took the woman and man."

"They?" Bay, Brodie, and Colt asked at the same time.

"How many?" Brodie asked.

Hunt shook his head. "Not until you guarantee I won't hang for what you think I've done."

Brodie looked at Colt, who rubbed the stubble on his chin. "As long as Hunt has information which helps us find them, we might be able to work something out with the judge."

Bay shot a frustrated gaze between the two lawmen. "Such as?"

"Could be the judge would go for a prison sentence," Colt replied.

"For life," Brodie answered.

"Hell no. I'm not spending my life in San Quentin."

The three whipped their gazes to Hunt, Colt the first to respond. "Death or life in prison. It's your decision."

Swallowing the knot in his throat, Hunt shook his head, not liking either choice.

August listened to the interaction, staying quiet. Few knew he'd been appointed as a federal judge for their region, able to hear cases when the regular circuit judge wouldn't be riding in for more than a couple weeks. It was one reason he'd been so eager to hire Griff MacKenzie.

"If I agree, how do you know the judge will accept our agreement?"

Colt, Brodie, and Bay turned toward August, waiting for his response.

Taking a couple steps forward, his expression hardened. "The judge will accept your agreement, as long as Suzette and Jasper are found."

Hunt hissed out a long string of curses. "There's no way I can guarantee you'll find them."

August shook his head. "Then I guess this is a waste of time."

Blowing out a frustrated breath, Hunt's mouth drew into a thin line. "You're sure the judge will agree?"

August nodded. "I am."

"How can you be so certain?"

A slight grin turned up the corners of August's mouth. "Because I'm the judge."

Suzette refused to show fear as she stared at the silhouette of a man she'd hoped never to see again. She'd thought Dave Calvan was out of her life forever, content with what he'd done to her and Bay in St. Louis. The nightmare hadn't ended.

He'd somehow found them in Conviction, and she had a good idea how. The newspaper article about Bay had appeared in San Francisco, Denver, Kansas City, and St Louis. And those were the places she knew about.

"What do you think they plan to do with us?" Jasper's scared voice pierced through her.

Like her, his hands and legs had been tied to a chair. He didn't deserve to be caught in the nightmare with her and Bay.

Leaning toward him, she lowered her voice. "Calvan is using us as bait to draw out Bay."

A sick expression passed over Jasper's face as he absorbed her words. Working to control the bile rising in his throat, he shook his head. "Bay is too smart not to know what Calvan plans."

"It won't matter. He'll still come for us." She knew that as well as she knew how much they loved each other. If it was within his power, Bay would never allow someone to hurt her. The realization of how much she trusted him whirled through her. He would come for them.

"Won't be long now."

Suzette glanced up to see Calvan standing over her. "What won't be much longer?"

"Donahue. I've sent him another message."

The pounding in her chest increased, but she didn't respond.

"He'll come for you. When he does, I'll allow you one last look at him before he takes his last breath."

Suzette wanted to scream. Instead, she took a long, calming breath. "You're a fool if you believe Bay will let you and your men live. You'll be in the ground before the sun sets."

If she hadn't been watching, Suzette would've missed the flinch passing over Calvan's face.

"Unlike in St. Louis, Bay will be ready for you." She lifted a brow. "Do you know how many jobs he's taken and not gotten who he was after?"

Calvan's nostrils flared. "No."

"None. It doesn't matter if it's one, two, three, or more. Bay always gets his prey."

Bending down, he got within inches of her face. "He won't be as lucky this time."

Lifting her chin, she smirked. "Luck has nothing to do with the way Bay will kill you." She shifted her gaze to the others. "All three of you."

Grabbing the hair at the back of her head, he tightened his grip until Suzette's eyes began to water. Calvan drew her face to no more than an inch from his, features twisting in rage.

"Leave her alone."

Calvan looked at Jasper, pulling his free hand back to deliver a hard slap to his face. "This is none of your business."

Tilting his head back to stave off the blood flowing from his nose, Jasper ignored the warning. Choking, he glowered at Calvan. "I'm making it my business. Believe me, you won't be hard for Bay to get the best of. Any man who uses a woman is no man at all."

Suzette grimaced at Jasper's words, as well as the pain when Calvan tightened his grip on her hair. She hadn't expected Jasper to defend her in a way which would cause the outlaw to lash out at him. In fact, she hadn't expected much at all from the efficient, quiet law assistant. A man she'd never seen wear a gun.

Calvan lifted his hand to strike Jasper again when a shout from one of his men stopped him.

"Dave, we have to get going if we're going to reach the meeting place before Donahue."

Dropping his hand from Suzette's hair, he stepped away. "I'll deal with the two of you when we get back." Calvan started to turn away, then stopped. "Once Bay and anyone with him are dead."

Before leaving for the location the outlaws described in the latest message, August had sent a rider to the MacLaren ranch, letting them know of the kidnapping. And that the wedding had been postponed. By the time the second message arrived, Colin, Quinn, Fletcher, and Bram had joined them.

Colin and Bram had made the mistake of checking on Camden, finding him more than ready to leave, over the doctor's objection.

"I'm going with you." Camden struggled to pull on his clothes, determined not to be left behind.

"Nae. You're not going anywhere, lad." Colin yanked the shirt from his brother's hand.

"Aye, I am," Camden shot back, tearing the shirt from Colin's grasp. "Will you be helping me or be in my way?"

Bram moved beside him. "Ach. You're in no condition to ride out, Cam. Listen to Colin and stay here."

"You're not understanding. I need to be doing something instead of lying here."

Bay had stepped inside the clinic a minute before, understanding the scene before him. "I need you to stay with Suzette's friend, Evangeline." He held up his hand when Camden opened his mouth to protest. "Vangie's in a panic. She's never been in the middle of anything like this, much less a kidnapping. I'd appreciate it if you would stay with her, keep her safe."

Camden knew it was a bad idea for him to be alone with Vangie, a woman he'd had an immediate attraction to when they'd met at the Great West Café. Still, he wouldn't refuse Bay.

"Assuming the lass wants me there."

"She will." Bay looked between Colin and Bram. "He'll need help getting there."

"I can walk," Camden objected. "My shoulder was shot, not my leg."

"I'll be going with him, Colin." Bram helped Camden, who no longer seemed inclined to argue, slip into his shirt.

Bay rubbed a hand across his forehead. "We still haven't received instructions on what they want us to do next." The strained sound of his voice had the others looking at him. "If he lays a hand on her..." He couldn't finish, the thought of losing Suzette after all they'd been through crushing him.

Colin placed a hand on his shoulder. "We'll find her and Jasper, lad. And we'll be getting the men who took them."

Bay glanced at his friend, praying he was right.

Removing his hat, Camden met Vangie's gaze when she opened the door, eyes widening. "Um, Mr. MacLaren. It's, um...good to see you."

Seeing the redness in her eyes, he hesitated a moment before explaining. "Miss Rousseau. Bay Donahue sent me to stay here with you. I'm hoping it's all right." He wished Bram had stayed a few minutes longer, but his cousin had been anxious to get back with the other men.

She bit her lower lip, brows scrunching together. "I'm certain it isn't proper for the two of us to be in the house alone."

"Lass, it would be highly improper for you to be waiting here alone for Suzette's return." Camden sucked in a slow breath at the pain in his shoulder.

Seeing the brief anguish on his face, Vangie moved aside. "Please, come inside. I'll worry about consequences later."

He flashed her a grin as he stepped inside. "We'll be worrying about it together, lass."

Vangie's stomach fluttered at his words. She knew it would be hard having Camden in the house, a man she'd found appealing the first time they'd met, minutes before he'd been shot. Doubting he'd remember her sitting beside his bed in the clinic, holding his hand as he worked through a fitful sleep, she shut the door, clenching her hands in front of her.

"May I offer you coffee or tea?" Biting her lower lip again, she glanced around. "There's also whiskey."

He remembered Doc Tilden's warning to stay away from alcohol a few more days. "Coffee would be good."

Camden watched her walk into the kitchen, following the sway of her hips, the silky shine of her deep red hair. He knew once the redness on her face disappeared, he'd see bright blue, inquisitive eyes, the same ones which had drawn him to her before the shooting.

Following her to the kitchen, he rested a shoulder against the jamb, watching as she made coffee. "How are you doing, lass?"

She glanced at him over her shoulder. "I'll be better when they find Suzette." Straightening, Vangie's gaze locked on his bandaged arm. "How's your shoulder?"

"Doing better," he ground out.

Reaching to grab two cups, she stopped, moving toward him. "You should sit down, Mr. MacLaren."

"Aye, but only if you call me Camden or Cam." A grin lifted the corners of his mouth, seeing a flush color her cheeks.

"All right, Camden. But you must call me Vangie."

He walked to the table in the kitchen, slowly lowering himself into a chair. Even with Tilden's warning, he'd refused to acknowledge how weak he'd still be. Camden had to wonder how much help he'd be if the outlaws came for Vangie. He'd do what was needed to keep her safe.

"Here you are." She placed a cup in front of him. "Would you care for sugar or some milk?"

"Black is fine, lass. Thank you." He waited to take a sip until she sat across from him, enjoying the first swallow of coffee since being shot.

Silence lay between them, Vangie not meeting his gaze, Camden watching her hands shake as she brought the cup to her lips.

"Bay, Brodie, and the rest of my family aren't going to let anything happen to her, Vangie. The outlaws made the mistake of taking her and the lad. They'll be the ones to suffer."

"I hope so." Slapping a hand over her mouth, she winced. The words had spewed out before she could stop them.

"I'll not be disagreeing with you, lass. Those miscreants deserve whatever they get."

Chapter Twenty-Three

"Those lads won't be getting out of this alive." Colin spit out the words as the group rode closer to the meeting place.

Half a mile down the trail, they broke into two groups, meaning to surround the outlaws. Brodie kept Hunt with his group, which included Bay, Griff, and Sam. Before they'd left the jail, Hunt admitted he believed Dave Calvan and two of his men were the ones who took Suzette and Jasper. The news didn't surprise Bay.

"We'll be doing this right, Bay." Brodie's hard gaze landed on his friend. "I'll not allow this to be a vigilante hunt." He also shot a warning look at Griff, who answered with a curt nod.

Bay didn't answer. He respected Brodie, knowing he had a job to do. If it contrasted with what Bay wanted, though, he wouldn't let friendship or any lawman get in the way of rescuing Suzette and Jasper. And it wouldn't stop him from doling out justice to Dave Calvan, the man who'd abducted them.

"Bay, did you hear me?"

"I heard you, Brodie." It wasn't a promise, and Bay knew the sheriff understood.

"Calvan won't be bringing the hostages with him."

Hunt's unexpected announcement had Brodie reining to a stop in front of him. "What do you mean?"

"Simple. They'll be at that shack he uses to store his weapons and supplies. My guess is he'll leave his woman," Hunt nodded at Bay, "and Jasper there until it's over. Even if he and his men die, you won't be able to find the hostages until they've starved to death or animals have taken care of them." He couldn't suppress an approving grin. "If he lives, he has Miss Gasnier to himself. It's quite brilliant, really. Of course, Calvan doesn't intend to die." Hunt sent a pointed look at Bay.

Brodie ignored the last, his jaw set. "Where is this cabin?"

Shrugging, Hunt gave a slow shake of his head. "If Calvan wins this little skirmish, you won't need the location. If he dies, I'll be happy to tell you."

Before Brodie realized what was happening, Bay launched himself out of his saddle at Hunt. The impact sent both men to the ground, where Bay slammed a fist into the outlaw's face.

"You'll tell us where the cabin is, or so help me God..." He lifted his arm to land another punch when Griff's hand clasped Bay's wrist.

"Enough. There's another way to work this out." Griff hauled him up, leaving Hunt to take care of himself, including the blood on his face, knowing he'd have a tough time with his hands tied in front of him. Griff glanced at an amused Brodie. "Were you just going to leave Bay to beat the answer out of him?"

"I'd have stopped it if I thought the lad intended to kill him." Brodie turned his attention to Hunt. "Before you mount up, you'll be telling me—" The sound of gunshots rang through the air, halting whatever else he intended to say.

"It's coming from the direction of Colin's group." Sam had already reined his horse toward the direction of the gunfire.

"Get on your horse, Hunt!" Brodie emphasized his order with a six-shooter pointed at the outlaw's chest. He shot a glance over his shoulder at the others. "Hold up."

The instant Hunt landed in the saddle, Brodie motioned for the group to ride out. The gunfire had subsided, but the lack of it didn't lessen the churning in everyone's stomach. Especially Bay's.

When he thought the gunfire had stopped, two more shots split the air, confirming the direction Sam had selected. Bay pushed his horse forward, passing Sam, unable to stay behind any longer. Calvan and his men were out there. So were the MacLarens. One group sought revenge against Bay, and he didn't intend to let them take it.

Charging to the edge of a clearing, he reined up. From the spot hidden within the trees, his gaze darted over the nearby trees and rock formations. A sharp whistle drew his attention, as well as that of the other men who'd stopped around him.

"It's our lads." Brodie recognized the unique call perfected by most of the MacLarens. Putting fingers to his mouth, he returned the whistle. An instant later, he heard a quick response, followed by a more intricate whistle. Brodie's teeth ground together. "One of the lads is hurt. Another is making his way toward us. We're to stay here."

Bay arched a brow. "You understood all that from a few calls?"

The corners of Brodie's mouth lifted. "Aye. We've more if you want to hear them sometime."

Sam would've chuckled if the reason for them sitting atop their horses at this spot wasn't so serious. "When this is over, you'll want to take Brodie up on his offer. It's a real education."

A crackling in the brush stopped Bay's response. Instead, he pulled his gun, as did the others, the group allowing their gazes to move over the area behind them. Staying as still as an alerted deer, they watched, no one moving a muscle.

A low whistle preceded a man striding from behind the trees, his hands held up.

Bay blew out a slow breath. "It's Quinn."

Sam kicked his horse forward, holding out a hand so he could swing up behind him. Quinn set his gaze on his cousin, Brodie.

"Calvan and his lads are hidden in the rocks. They have us pinned down. One of their shots clipped August on the leg, but the lad's doing fine. I've never heard such a long stream of cursing." Quinn shook his head. "Colin wants us to go around behind them and wait for his signal."

"How many men?" Bay asked.

"Three for certain. Maybe four," Quinn responded. He shot a look at Hunt. "We should be sending him out to draw fire."

Ev straightened in his saddle, opening his mouth to protest, when bullets rained around them. His horse bucked, knocking him from the saddle and onto his injured right arm. The outlaw didn't attempt to stop the roar of pain. The sound brought another round of gunfire, most hitting the ground, some chipping at tree limbs.

Bay and the others slid from their horses, taking refuge wherever they could, leaving Hunt rolling on the ground. When the shots stalled, Brodie and Bay dashed out, hauling the outlaw into the brush. Before Hunt could gather his breath, Bay leaned down, his face red with rage.

"Where is the cabin?" A smirk appeared on Hunt's face before Bay slapped it away, his gun inches from the outlaw's face. "You've got three seconds." Cocking the gun, he waited.

Hunt's eyes widened an instant before he blew out a curse. He nodded south. "It's less than half a mile down the Feather River from here, on the east side. It's surrounded by trees and rocks. Hard to get to. You'll never find it by yourself, especially with the sun setting."

Bay straightened, shaking off Hunt's warning before glancing at Brodie. "I'm going after her."

"Not by yourself, lad."

Griff crouched low, moving closer to them. "I'll go with him. Will you have enough men if we leave?"

Brodie nodded. "Three of them. Seven of us. Aye. We'll be fine. Be watching in case Calvan left a man behind with Suzette and Jasper."

"We'll go that way." Griff nodded to a trail leading away from the shooters.

Leaving Brodie with Hunt, Sam, and Quinn, they found their horses, mounting quickly before riding into the approaching darkness.

Suzette's chest rose and fell, the continuing band of worry tightening to a painful degree. Her head pounded, and if her hands hadn't been tied, she knew they'd be shaking.

It had been well over an hour since the gunmen had ridden out, leaving her and Jasper alone. No water. No food. They'd been given nothing since arriving at the old shack. It wasn't the thirst or hunger bothering her. At least they'd left the door open, allowing somewhat of a breeze to cool the stifling air inside.

Knowing Calvan had gone after Bay spurred a pain in her heart no amount of wishful thinking could lessen. Suzette's mind told her the outlaws didn't stand a chance against Bay. No one ever had, and she doubted his luck would change now. Although it hadn't been luck that had made him successful as a hired gun.

Skill and experience had made him of great value to landowners and others who desired someone to rid them of rustlers and thieves. Bay had always made certain the men he went after were outlaws, not just an inconvenience to the rich and powerful.

Calvan wasn't rich or powerful, but he had taken something more important than Bay's own life. She knew he'd do anything to find and rescue her. Even if it meant putting himself in front of a bullet.

"Jasper?"

"Yes."

"Are you doing all right?" She cursed the fact Calvan had moved their chairs back-to-back, making it impossible to see the other's face.

"Fine. I'm working on loosening the rope around my wrists. A few more minutes and I should have them off. Then I'll get us both out of here."

Suzette forced herself not to feel too much hope. "I've been trying to do the same, but mine won't budge."

"I'm not surprised. Calvan tightened yours before he left, but not mine."

Silence fell over them. Other than the sound of Jasper tugging at the rope, the small cabin was quiet, the same as it had been since the outlaws rode out. A few minutes later, Jasper let out a low sound of triumph.

"Got them. I need to get them off my ankles, then I'll work on yours."

Suzette held her breath, praying they were close to getting away from Calvan and the fate he planned for them. Hearing Jasper's chair being pushed away, she felt his fingers working on the rope around her wrists. Her shoulders began to relax an instant before a loud swish had her tensing. A scream lodged in her throat when a blazing torch shot through the open doorway, landing a few feet away.

"Ah hell." Jasper shoved his bindings away, pushing her chair away from the fire. A moment later, he tilted the chair back, trying to drag it out the door. Hearing another loud swishing sound, he froze as another torch passed by them, landing close to the first one. He dragged the chair away from the door, frantically searching for another way out. "We've got to get out of here."

"But someone's out there." Suzette felt certain Calvan had thrown the burning orbs into the dilapidated shack. Before she could voice it, bullets hit the few remaining windows, showering them with glass.

Jasper shouted a few more curses, louder this time. The flames had taken hold on the rough-hewn floor, smoke spreading enough to choke them.

Spotting the water bucket, he tore off his shirt, tearing it in two, plunging both inside. Wringing one out, he dashed back to Suzette.

"Lean your head back," he choked out, placing the wet cloth over her face. Bending, he continued to choke while working on the rope on her wrists, then her ankles. After tugging hard, they gave way at the same time more gunshots sounded. This time, they didn't hit the cabin.

Unable to draw in a breath, Jasper grabbed the other half of his shirt from the bucket, not sparing the time to wring it out before putting it to his face. His eyes stung from the smoke, his skin searing from the heat. Tossing the shirt onto the flames, he picked up the bucket, pouring what was left onto the fire. Jasper stilled at the sound of Bay's hard voice.

"Calvan! It's just you and me. Show yourself."

Gunshots followed the shouted order. Seconds later, Griff launched himself into the cabin, rolling to the side, aiming his gun out the open doorway. Glancing around, his gaze landed on Suzette.

"Hello, Suz." Griff's brief grin disappeared as he choked on the thick smoke. "We have to get you two out of here. Bay's going to draw Calvan's fire."

"But how—"

Before she got the rest out, Griff grabbed her hand, almost dragging her against the wall near the door. "Stay with us, Jasper. Both of you stay low. This is going to happen fast." Shielding them with his body, Griff inched closer to the door, his gun held in front of him. "Ready?" He didn't wait for their response before counting to three.

Grip tightening on Suzette's hand, Griff fired toward the direction where he'd last seen Calvan. Bullets pelted the ground around them as they ran toward where Bay fired from behind a dense stand of brush. They almost made it.

A groan had Suzette glancing behind her. "Jasper," she cried out, trying to pull Griff to a stop.

"I'll get him once you're safe with Bay, Suz." Dragging her behind him, Griff continued firing, bursting through the brush.

An unwelcome sob escaped her at the sight of Bay, but he didn't stop firing or acknowledge her in any way. She understood why. All his concentration needed to be on Calvan, keeping him occupied while Griff went back for Jasper.

"Stay down, Suz. You ready for me to get Jasper, Bay?"

Again, Bay didn't move from his crouched position, refusing to break his focus. "Ready."

Griff fired first, waiting for Bay to follow before storming from the dense cover toward Jasper. Grabbing his collar, Griff hauled him back to the brush while continuing to fire. A ragged groan came from Jasper. At least he was alive. For now.

A bullet whizzed past Griff's head, provoking an explosion of expletives. Quickening his pace, he used all his strength to drag him into the cover of the brush. Holstering his weapon, Griff turned his attention to Jasper, seeing the wound on his thigh. Taking out his knife, he ripped the pants open, applying pressure on the injury. Shifting, he noticed Suzette crawl next to them.

Kneeling next to Griff, Suzette didn't hesitate to lift her skirt, tearing strips of cloth from her chemise. "Jasper, can you hear me?" The words were whispered, meant to be soothing as she began working on his wound. Both she and Griff had noticed it was a graze, although a deep one requiring sutures. She leaned closer to his ear. "Jasper?"

"He's out cold, sweetheart." Bay's voice rolled over her at the same time his hands rested on her shoulders. "Will you be all right tending to him?"

Dread ripped through her. "Why?" She hated that her voice shook.

Bay wanted to wrap his arms around her, kiss her until neither of them could draw a breath. Instead, he dropped his hands from her shoulders.

"Griff and I are going after Calvan. It's been quiet for close to a minute. Plenty of time for him to ride out."

Closing her eyes for an instant, she glanced over her shoulder. "Then go. I'll be fine here with Jasper."

"Here." Bay handed her his extra pistol. "Use this if you spot any sign of Calvan."

Taking it, she swallowed. "All right. But please, be careful."

Brushing a kiss over her mouth, he moved toward Griff. "I will."

Bay went left, Griff right as each made their way through the thick stand of trees and low brush. Their paths appeared to be hidden by low, green branches and clusters of large boulders.

Until a shot broke away a slice of rock above Bay's head. Another one hit close to the same place a moment later.

Shifting so his back was against the rock, he held his gun ready. Most men were better with rifles, using six-shooters when accuracy wasn't as critical. Bay had always been equally lethal with both.

"You won't get me, Donahue."

Bay didn't respond. He took the brief pause to move around the boulder to come up behind where he expected Calvan to be. Griff would be doing the same from the other direction.

"And you won't save your woman and Jasper. You may have gotten them out of the burning cabin, but they won't survive the rest of the day. It's too bad she left the office with the young man. My problem is with you."

Bay wanted to yell back, ask Calvan to let them go and deal with him. Yelling would only give away his location and he had to allow Griff time to come up on the other side. Once he gave the signal Calvan was in his sights, Bay would charge from his position.

A scream stalled his breath.

Chapter Twenty-Four

Suzette kept herself busy trying to stop Jasper's wound from bleeding. She'd used several strips from her chemise already, failing to do much to stem the flow. Applying one more strip, she rested both hands over the wound, pressing with all her strength.

Two shots had her resting back on her heels, fear rushing through her. Focusing on Jasper, she let out a shaky breath, continuing to push on the wound. Another shot stalled her movements for a fraction of a second. Suzette heard Calvan yell but couldn't make out the words. Bay didn't respond. When Calvan shouted again, she stiffened, holding her breath. Again, Bay stayed silent. She understood why.

"Donahue is a real fool to leave you behind again."

Suzette screamed, hearing the familiar voice. One of Calvan's men she recognized from St. Louis stood behind her, the barrel of his gun pushed against her head. Closing her eyes, she didn't stop pressing on Jasper's wound, glancing down at the gun in her lap.

Bay had taught her to use it not long after they married, insisting she practice at least once a week. Since moving to Conviction, her work provided little time to practice. Still, she hadn't forgotten anything he'd taught her.

"You're coming with me." The outlaw grabbed her hair, dragging Suzette away from Jasper.

"Let me go!" She reached up, slapping at his arm, but his grip tightened. "Stop!"

"Don't make me any madder than I am. Calvan's got your boys pinned down. Soon, they'll be dead and you'll be riding off with us."

Continuing to slap at his arm, she tried to dig her heels into the dirt, without success. The outlaw tugged harder, creating a blinding burn in Suzette's scalp. She refused to be used as bait to draw Bay or Griff out, knowing if she surrendered, they'd kill her and Jasper. Her death might not come right away, but it would come.

Anger welling inside, Suzette sucked in a deep breath before letting out an ear-piercing scream.

When Bay heard Suzette, he didn't waste a moment debating whether to stay in place or go to her side. Bending low, he raced away from the cover of the boulders, cringing when bullets pelted the ground around him.

Zigzagging as best as he could, Bay heard another scream, then Suzette shouting at someone. Drawing closer, he crouched down behind a tree, his blood running cold.

One of Calvan's men held her by the hair, his other hand coming down to land a blow to her face. Blood ran from her nose. Blinding rage tore through Bay. Waiting for Griff would be the smart choice. Instead, he lifted his gun, aiming.

A shot rang out, hitting the outlaw in the center of his forehead. Eyes wide in shock, the man let go of Suzette's hair as he fell backwards, landing prone on the ground.

She sucked in a relieved breath, not looking at the body or scanning the trees before scrambling back into their cover. Seeing Jasper's pale face, Suzette ripped another strip from her chemise, resuming her efforts to stop the bleeding. That was when she wondered who'd killed the outlaw.

It had to be Bay or Griff. She guessed it to be her husband, which told her Bay was still alive. She jerked at the renewed gunshots indicating the fight wasn't over. Suzette had understood Calvan had two men with him, but now realized he'd brought more. They hadn't been with them on the ride to the cabin, probably staying hidden so those coming after them wouldn't know how many they'd face.

At Jasper's low moan, she pressed a hand to his face, the skin cool to her touch. No fever. Yet.

"Jasper, can you hear me?"

Another moan slipped through his lips. "Water..."

Looking around, she hoped to find a canteen Bay or Griff may have left behind. "I'm sorry. There isn't any."

Eyes fluttering open, his glazed eyes met hers. "My leg."

"You were shot when Griff got us out of the cabin."

His eyes closed again, then opened. "Cabin?"

"Do you remember the fire?"

It took a moment as Jasper tried to recall what had happened. "Calvan." He bit the name out in disgust.

"Bay and Griff are going after him and his men, then we'll get you to town and to a doctor."

Trying to push himself up, he fell back on a flash of pain. "I should be helping them," he ground out.

"No. You need rest."

Both flinched at the sound of gunfire closing in on them. Her worried gaze flew to Jasper before she looked behind and around her.

"He's going into the trees behind the cabin, Griff!" Bay's shout sounded through the darkening night. Until that moment, Suzette hadn't noticed the gunfire had stopped. At least momentarily.

"I've got him," Griff yelled back.

Bay didn't reply, causing Suzette's heart to seize.

"You'll pay for killing my brother, Donahue. Nothing you do will save you from my kind of justice."

Bay had suspected what happened in St. Louis, the arsenic, and kidnapping of Suzette and Jasper had something to do with one of his past jobs. No man would do what Calvan had without good reason, even if it wasn't justified.

"Who's your brother?" Bay knew the answer, but needed time for Griff to move behind Calvan.

"I should've known a man like you wouldn't remember all the men you've killed. There's too damn many of them."

Bay stayed hidden, ignoring the intended insult, his focus fixed on the cabin and Griff's position. Calvan had brought more men with him than Hunt stated. Bay guessed at least three more, which included the one he'd shot for striking Suzette.

"What's his name?" Bay glanced around the corner of the cabin, seeing Griff motion to him. The movement let Bay know he had a clear shot at Calvan. Shaking his head, he warned Griff off. If anyone killed the outlaw, it would be him.

The sound of approaching horses drew Bay's attention. Riders coming up behind him. He prayed it was the MacLarens and August, not more of the outlaws.

Moving farther into the cover of the trees, he waited, sending a warning look at Suzette, placing a finger over his lips. Nodding, she hovered over Jasper, doing her best to protect him from additional injury. She knew it meant little. Outlaws wouldn't care if they shot through her and Jasper. Calvan wanted Bay. Her death would mean little. She'd still do everything possible to shield Jasper.

Bay had no time to count the number of riders. He didn't need to. Relief washed over him at the sight of Brodie, Colin, and the rest of the men. They reined to a stop well before the burning cabin. The flames were almost out, but smoke continued to swirl upward. The fireplace and stove were still visible, although charred from the fire.

"Calvan's riding off, Bay!" Griff ran around to the front of what was left of the cabin. "He ran when he heard the horses coming this way."

Bay came out from his hiding place, waving off the group of riders as he hurried toward Griff. "Anyone with him?"

"Not that I could see." Griff nodded at Brodie, Colt, and Colin, who'd slipped from their horses to join them.

"We shot two of Calvan's lads." Brodie took an appraising look around, glancing at the dead outlaw on the ground.

"Calvan's alone. Rode out a couple minutes ago. We need to go after him." Bay holstered his gun, nodding toward the bushes. "Suzette is over there with Jasper. He was shot attempting to get out of the burning cabin. I'll need you to stay with them."

The sheriff motioned for Quinn. When he joined them, Brodie explained, pointing to the bushes to see Suzette peeking out. "We'll be needing lads to stay with them."

Quinn shifted, studying the men still on their horses. "August and Bram. The rest of us can go after Calvan."

"No." All eyes locked on Bay. "Griff and I will go."

Brodie shook his head. "Nae, lad. You'll not be going just the two of you." He looked at Colt. "You, Seth, and I will be going."

"We don't need five men, Brodie," Bay protested.

"Neither of you are lawmen. I'll not be letting you go without us."

Quinn looked at his cousin. "We should be going with you lads."

Shaking his head again, Brodie didn't change his mind. "Nae. You'll protect the others in case more of Calvan's men are around."

Quinn didn't like it, but nodded in agreement. "I'll let the other lads know."

"Suzette needs water and whiskey to clean Jasper's wound," Bay said.

"Aye. I'll make certain she gets them." Quinn walked off, going straight to Suzette and Jasper. Bay was right behind him.

Ducking under the branches, his chest squeezed when his gaze landed on her. Face smudged with soot and dirt, blood-soaked strips of her chemise lying on the ground around her, many men wouldn't find her attractive. To Bay, Suzette was the most beautiful woman in the world. And she was his.

Kneeling beside her, he brushed a kiss across her lips. "We're going after Calvan." The words were just out of his mouth when gunfire erupted from behind the cabin. "Stay here." Rushing out, Quinn beside him, they drew their guns, seeing Griff and Brodie ride out.

"Who fired the shots?" Quinn asked Colt when he reined up beside him.

"Calvan. He must've returned, hoping to get a shot off at Bay." Colt didn't explain further before kicking his horse to follow, Seth right behind him.

Cursing, Bay whistled for Spartacus, swinging into the saddle the instant his stallion stopped. Not looking back, he pressed the heels of his boots into the horse's sides. Gunshots rang out ahead of him. He swore fluently, realizing he might not be the one to bring down Calvan.

A few minutes passed before he caught up with Colt. Griff and Brodie were somewhere ahead of them, out of sight. Renewed gunfire had him kicking Spartacus again, his desire not to miss the kill spurring him on.

The sound of gunfire continued, then stopped. An eerie silence blanketed the air around Bay and Colt, the tension increasing. Slowing, both looked around, deciding which way to ride. They didn't have to wait long.

Griff and Brodie rode toward them, a body slung over the saddle of the horse behind them. A rush of curses spewed from Bay when he realized the body was Calvan's. Griff reined to within inches of him.

"Before you shoot me, Calvan had me in his sights. He didn't expect me to react as fast as I did." Griff leaned closer, not wanting Brodie or Colt to hear. "Besides, you've got enough kills on your conscience. Let this one rest in mine."

Bay had interrupted Doc Tilden's sleep to tend August's and Jasper's gunshot wounds before checking on Suzette. He'd paced the entire time.

Brodie and Sam made certain the injured men got home. August to his house, and Jasper to his room in the boardinghouse. When Tilden gave his approval for Bay to take Suzette home, he put an arm around her shoulders, tucking her against him as they walked home.

Walking up the steps, he opened the door, scooping her into his arms to cross the threshold. She wrapped her arms around his neck before looking around. One light remained on in the quiet house.

"Vangie must be in bed. After all, it is close to midnight." She settled her face against his chest.

"Cam must also be in bed."

His comment had her pulling back. Her brows drew together. "Camden MacLaren?"

"Vangie was frantic. I asked him to stay with her until we returned."

The corners of her mouth slipped into a grin. "Is that so?"

Lowering his head, Bay kissed the sensitive spot below her ear, trailing his lips down her neck, feeling her shiver before he straightened.

Turning toward the stairs, he carried her to her bedroom, shoving the door open, then kicking it closed.

Bay set her down next to the bed, cupping her face in both hands. The kiss was slow and languid, his tongue tracing the silky fullness of her lips. Suzette's hands stroked up his arms, resting on his shoulders before slipping around his neck. In seconds, the kiss became urgent, more aggressive.

Adjusting his position, he wrapped both arms around her, needing to feel her against him. Having her in his arms, her mouth open for his, sent waves of heat rushing through him. He tugged her closer, leaving no space between them. Hearing her moan, he let his hands move to the buttons on the back of her dress, releasing them with a minimum of effort.

Another moan escaped when he slid the dress down her shoulders. He let his lips trace a path of hot kisses down her neck, along her shoulder, to the swell of her breasts. Lifting his head, he stared into lust glazed eyes, her mouth swollen with his kisses.

"I won't be leaving tonight, or any other night, sweetheart." He bent, brushing another kiss over her moist lips. "I love you more than my own life, more than I ever thought possible."

Lowering his head, he covered her mouth with his, creating a fire that flared between them.

"Bay, please..."

Chuckling against her lips, he shoved the dress and chemise to the floor, letting his hands wander over her soft skin. "I desire you more than you'll ever know. You're my entire world, Suzette. Tonight, I'm going to show you in every way possible how much you mean to me."

Epilogue

One week later...

Unlike the wedding they'd first planned—small, with a few friends—this one filled the church. All the MacLarens attended, as did Brodie's deputies and a good number of townsfolk they'd met over their time in Conviction, including both doctors.

Griff stood next to Bay, Vangie next to Suzette. She couldn't help noticing how her friend took quick, furtive glances over her shoulder at Camden, her face flushing when he met her gaze. The actions amused Suzette. Perhaps something was starting between the two.

August sat in the front row next to Kyla MacLaren, their hands entwined, the cane he hated using resting against the bench. Audrey MacLaren, her son, Quinn, and his wife, Emma, occupied the rest of the row. Behind them, Camden sat with Colin, his wife, Sarah, and more MacLarens.

When the reverend pronounced them man and wife, Bay took advantage, bending Suzette over his arm for a searing kiss. The action caused the crowd to applaud and cheer, sealing the joy Bay and Suzette felt. Walking past the rows, she couldn't help noticing the flush on Vangie's face, or Camden's eyes locked on her. Suzette found herself wondering how close they'd become while waiting for Bay to rescue her.

Reaching the back of the church, Bay took her hand in his, bending down to brush another kiss across her lips. "I love you."

"I love you, too, Bay."

"All right. Enough of that, lad." Brodie clasped his shoulder.

Laughing, Bay shook his outstretched hand, then those of several others, while Suzette was engulfed by several women. "We should get to the restaurant. I hope there are enough tables and chairs."

"Ach, don't worry about it, lad." Colin slapped him on the back. "We'll stand if necessary."

Another smile spread across Bay's face. "There will be plenty of food and a huge cake."

"Cake?" Bram's brows flickered in amusement.

"Biggest darn thing you've ever seen. Suzette refused to have our wedding without it." His eyes wandered to her. "I'd better get my bride so we can all head to the restaurant. The new man, Zeke, will be wondering about us."

"I've met him. Seems to be a good man." Brodie let his gaze move over the crowd.

Bay nodded. "He's a mystery, but I do believe Suzette made a good decision in hiring him."

"Enough of this talk. I'm hungry."

Bay chuckled at Brodie's grin. "You're right." Walking to the group of women, he threaded his fingers through Suzette's. "Time to feed these people, sweetheart." Placing an almost chaste kiss on her cheek, he tugged her outside, leading them to the restaurant.

Within minutes, all chairs were occupied, servers moving from one table to the next, filling glasses with champagne. Suzette couldn't keep the smile from her face. Since returning from her ordeal, numerous friends and people she'd never met stopped by the restaurant to ask about her. For the first time, she truly felt as if she belonged.

Her gaze lit on Vangie at a table next to theirs. Camden sat on one side of her with Griff on the other. Suzette couldn't stop herself from wondering if both men held an interest in her beautiful friend. She watched as Camden leaned close to Vangie, her friend smiling at whatever he said, a blush coloring her cheeks. Suzette no longer wondered if the two were attracted to each other. She did, however, wonder at Griff's interest.

Suzette's attention shifted to the entrance when the front door burst open. A man dressed in dusty black pants, coat, and hat stood there. Above average in height, his shoulders were broad, arms thick, straining the fabric of his coat.

"Do you know him?" Bay asked as the man took several steps inside.

"No." The word had just left her lips when Suzette heard Vangie gasp. Glancing at her, she saw her friend lean toward Camden, as if for protection, her hand covering her mouth, eyes wide. In fright or surprise, Suzette didn't know. Either way, she knew Vangie recognized him.

Bay pushed back his chair and stood at the same time Brodie began walking toward the man.

"I'm Sheriff MacLaren. Are you here for Bay and Suzette?"

The man shot Brodie a cursory glance, not answering before searching the faces in the room.

Brodie tried again. "The restaurant is closed for a wedding celebration."

Not finding who he sought, the man looked back at him for an instant. Turning toward the crowd, he opened his mouth, his loud voice vibrating throughout the room.

"I've come for Evangeline Rousseau and won't be leaving without her."

Thank you for taking the time to read Bay's Desire. If you enjoyed it, please consider telling your friends or posting a short review. Word of mouth is an author's best friend and much appreciated.

Watch for book nine in the MacLarens of Boundary Mountain series, Cam's Hope.

Please join my reader's group to be notified of my New Releases at: https://www.shirleendavies.com/contact-me.html

I care about quality, so if you find something in error, please contact me via email at shirleen@shirleendavies.com

About the Author

Shirleen Davies writes romance—historical and contemporary western romance with a touch of suspense. She is the best-selling author of the MacLarens of Fire Mountain Series, the MacLarens of Boundary Mountain Series, and the Redemption Mountain Series. Shirleen grew up in Southern California, attended Oregon State University, and has degrees from San Diego State University and the University of Maryland. Her passion is writing emotionally charged stories of flawed people who find redemption through love and acceptance. She lives with her husband in a beautiful town in northern Arizona. Between them, they have five adult sons who are their greatest achievements.

I love to hear from my readers!

Send me an email: shirleen@shirleendavies.com
Visit my Website: www.shirleendavies.com
Sign up to be notified of New Releases:
www.shirleendavies.com
Check out all of my Books:
www.shirleendavies.com/books.html
Comment on my Blog:
www.shirleendavies.com/blog.html
Follow me on Amazon:
http://www.amazon.com/author/shirleendavies

Follow my on BookBub:
https://www.bookbub.com/authors/shirleen-davies

Other ways to connect with me:

Facebook Author Page:
http://www.facebook.com/shirleendaviesauthor
Twitter: www.twitter.com/shirleendavies
Pinterest: http://pinterest.com/shirleendavies
Instagram:
https://www.instagram.com/shirleendavies_author/
Google Plus:
https://plus.google.com/+ShirleenDaviesAuthor

Books by Shirleen Davies
Historical Western Romance Series
MacLarens of Fire Mountain

Tougher than the Rest, Book One
Faster than the Rest, Book Two
Harder than the Rest, Book Three
Stronger than the Rest, Book Four
Deadlier than the Rest, Book Five
Wilder than the Rest, Book Six

Redemption Mountain

Redemption's Edge, Book One
Wildfire Creek, Book Two
Sunrise Ridge, Book Three
Dixie Moon, Book Four
Survivor Pass, Book Five
Promise Trail, Book Six
Deep River, Book Seven
Courage Canyon, Book Eight
Forsaken Falls, Book Nine
Solitude Gorge, Book Ten
Rogue Rapids, Book Eleven
Restless Wind, Coming next in the series!

MacLarens of Boundary Mountain

Colin's Quest, Book One,
Brodie's Gamble, Book Two
Quinn's Honor, Book Three
Sam's Legacy, Book Four
Heather's Choice, Book Five
Nate's Destiny, Book Six
Blaine's Wager, Book Seven
Fletcher's Pride, Book Eight
Bay's Desire, Book Nine
Cam's Hope, Book Ten, Coming next in the
series!

Contemporary Romance Series

MacLarens of Fire Mountain

Second Summer, Book One
Hard Landing, Book Two
One More Day, Book Three
All Your Nights, Book Four
Always Love You, Book Five
Hearts Don't Lie, Book Six
No Getting Over You, Book Seven
'Til the Sun Comes Up, Book Eight
Foolish Heart, Book Nine
Forever Love, Book Ten, Coming next in the
series!

Peregrine Bay

Reclaiming Love, Book One, A Novella
Our Kind of Love, Book Two

Burnt River

Shane's Burden, Book One by Peggy Henderson
Thorn's Journey, Book Two by Shirleen Davies
Aqua's Achilles, Book Three by Kate Cambridge
Ashley's Hope, Book Four by Amelia Adams
Harpur's Secret, Book Five by Kay P. Dawson
Mason's Rescue, Book Six by Peggy L. Henderson
Del's Choice, Book Seven by Shirleen Davies
Ivy's Search, Book Eight by Kate Cambridge
Phoebe's Fate, Book Nine by Amelia Adams
Brody's Shelter, Book Ten by Kay P. Dawson
Boone's Surrender, Book Eleven by Shirleen Davies
Watch for more books in the series!

The best way to stay in touch is to subscribe to my newsletter. Go to www.shirleendavies.com and subscribe in the box at the top of the right column that asks for your email. You'll be notified of new books before they are released, have chances to win great prizes, and receive other subscriber-only specials.